THE ROYAL FIRST IRREGULARS

It's a story about morality, about sacrifice, about what people want from life. It's a fun story–there's quips, swordfights, chases through the streets. It's a compelling, convincing work of fantasy, and a worthy addition to the rich tapestry that is the works of Maradaine.

— SCI-FI AND FANTASY REVIEWS

Marshall Ryan Maresca is one of the most ambitious fantasy authors to burst on the scene in the last decade.

— BLACK GATE MAGAZINE

Maresca continues his expert expansion of his intricately-crafted world, introducing fascinating new locations and vibrant characters while serving up a high-energy, magic-laced plot. *The Mystical Murders of Yin Mara* is a clever, captivating adventure.

— CASS MORRIS, AUTHOR OF
FROM UNSEEN FIRE

ALSO BY
MARSHALL RYAN MARESCA

MARADAINE SAGA PHASE ONE

The Thorn of Dentonhill
The Alchemy of Chaos
The Imposters of Aventil

A Murder of Mages
An Import of Intrigue
A Parliament of Bodies

The Holver Alley Crew
Lady Henterman's Wardrobe
The Fenmere Job

Way of the Shield
Shield of the People
People of the City

THE DISPLACED DAUGHTERS
An Unintended Voyage

MARADAINE SAGA PHASE TWO

The Assassins of Consequence
The New King of Rose Street*

An Unkindness of Uncircled Mages*
A Pride of Partners*

The Quarrygate Gambit
The Andrendon Plan*

City of the Truth*
Truth of the Crown*

MARADAINE SAGA SHORTS
The Mystical Murders of Yin Mara
Hultiehia
The Withered Boy
The Royal First Irregulars
A Proper Lady of Society*

THE ZIAPARR CYCLE
The Velocity of Revolution

*- Forthcoming

THE ROYAL FIRST IRREGULARS

MARADAINE SAGA STORY
BOOK FOUR

MARSHALL RYAN MARESCA

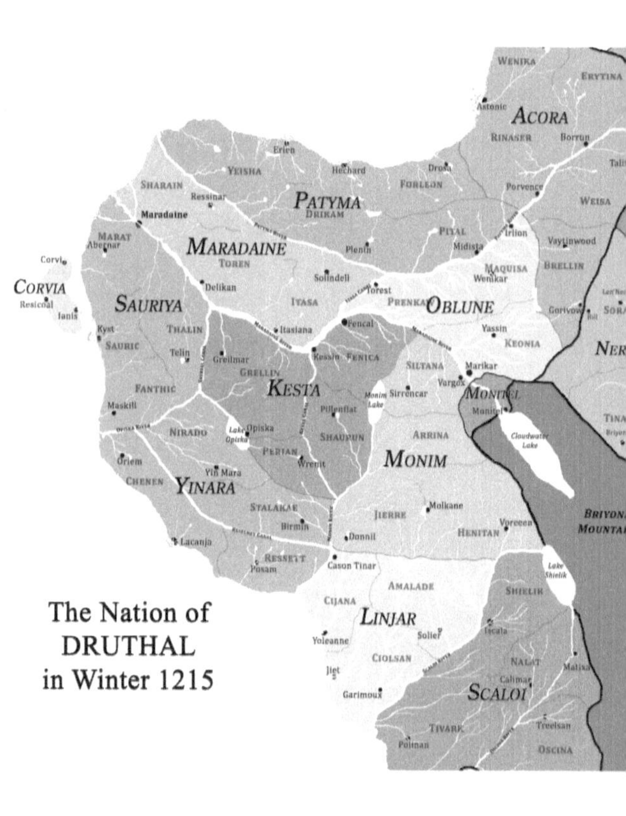

The Nation of
DRUTHAL
in Winter 1215

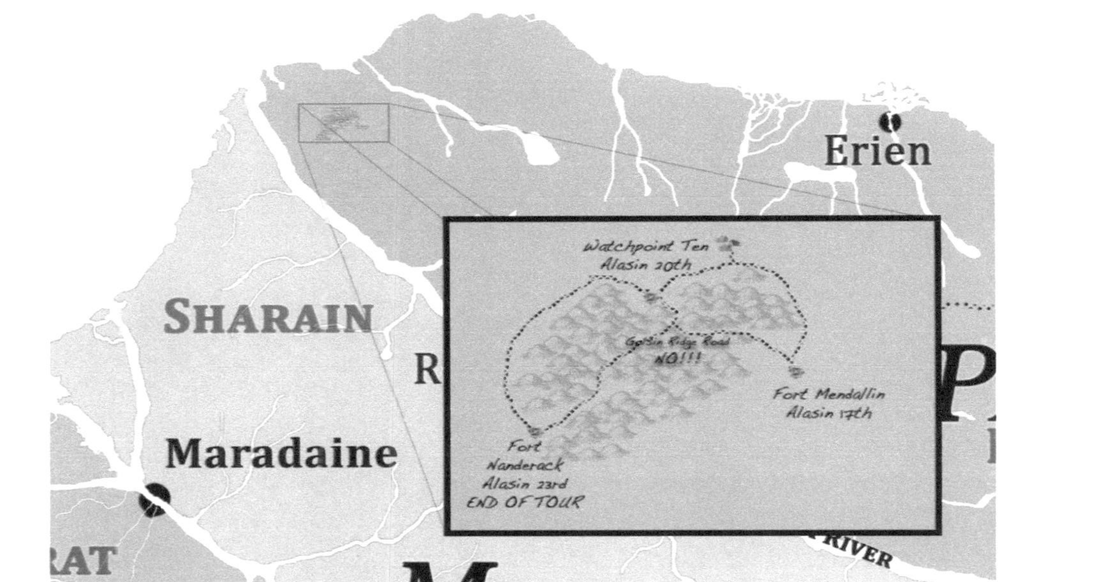

SHARAIN
Maradaine
Erien
RAT
RIVER
R
P
Watchpoint Ten
Alasin 20th
Goblin Ridge Road
NO.111
Fort Mendallin
Alasin 17th
Fort
Nanderack
Alasin 23rd
END OF TOUR

LIEUTENANT FREDELLE PENCE WAS AS ready as she could be.

Uniform on, weapon in hand, and the enemy…oh, the enemy was right there, waiting for her. She hadn't seen them yet, but she could hear them, howling like animals. She didn't want to see them, to have to look in their eyes those hungry, terrible eyes, every one of those bastards. She could do what she needed without looking at them. She could do it with her eyes closed. She and her team were ready, long hours training for this. Blazes, they were trained to do so much more.

She looked to her team. "Are we set?"

"How many you figure are out there?" Kelvanne asked her. Lieutenant Kelvanne Brownson, country girl from Oblune, an absolute tornado with the Oblunic pike. Learned from her father and grandfather, her ancestry deep with the pikemen. She didn't look nervous about what they were about to face. Never did. She looked angry. She should. Kelvanne was so much better than this. They all were.

"At least two hundred," Evicka said, her accent thick as honey. "Maybe more in the shadows." Lieutenant Evicka Renn was running her fingers along the chain of her Linjari flail, a wicked grin crossing her face while her dark eyes told a whole story of how she wanted to use her weapon tonight.

"All hungry for our flesh," Kelvanne said.

"Same as every other night," Fredelle said. "So let's do it. We're ready, Captain."

Captain Jacia Olmen, their commander—at least officially by rank—nodded and strode out into the light.

"Hello, boys," she called out. "Here's what you've been waiting for! The lovely ladies of the Royal First Irregulars!"

"Big smiles, ladies!" Fredelle didn't note who said it, but it was probably Raxi or Maxlynne. They still seemed to enjoy doing the performances. "Let's go!"

Fredelle took the lead, marching out on stage while twirling her quarterstaff.

"Hello, Fort Mendallin!" she called out as she took her place in the center. "Hope you're ready for a show!"

The crowd of the rank-and-file soldiers of Fort Mendallin all started hooting and hollering. Saints, given how isolated in northern Druthal this place was, how completely lacking in basic amenities, it was entirely possible they were the first women these boys had seen in months.

Fredelle forced a wide smile on her face. She just had to do the best show she had in her and get through this night.

———————————

THE ENTIRE SHOW WAS MUSCLE MEMORY FOR Fredelle. Every twirl, every parry, every step, every word. But she had nine women on stage with her. The choreography gave them no room for error. A few inches off their mark, and someone was taking a nasty crack across the head, or worse.

That was why Fredelle insisted they'd drill, they'd step through every one of their fights every night before performance. Even if the other ladies would grumble, she insisted. They were out there on stage with real weapons; they had to treat what they were doing with care and dignity.

"From the Archduchy of Maradaine, trained in the traditional weapon of the quarterstaff, Lieutenant Fredelle Pence!" Captain Olmen called out.

"She can handle my staff!" one of the soldiers out front called out. It was such a predictable heckle, Fredelle considered it part of the script. Some fool always said it, every night, thinking he was clever.

She was used to the catcalls and whistles, after all. It happened without fail, and it happened to every one of the ladies when they were on stage. It would happen even if they weren't wearing absurd variations on the Druth Army uniform, altered to high-slit knee-length skirts and coats tailored to button tight around the waist.

They were dressed like school girls, not soldiers.

That was the costume for the show. Fredelle accepted that. She had accepted this position, knowing exactly what it was. She was here to be a show pony, a pretty thing for troop morale.

As always happened, Captain Olmen continued with her speech without even a flinch.

"The quarterstaff's traditional use in the Archduchy of Maradaine dates back to before establishment of the Druth Throne, as the Kenalian Order formed nearly five hundred years before the Free Era. Fredelle's techniques and training date back to that ancient order, a noble legacy of our history before the Order and its techniques were integrated into the Druth Army!"

Fredelle finished her flourish and froze in a fighting pose as the next Irregular came out.

Of course, what Captain Olmen said wasn't exactly true. The Kenalians had been folded into the Tarian Order, not the Army. Fredelle had spent three years as an Initiate in the Tarian Order before she was passed over for Candidacy. When she was offered this placement in the Morale Division of the Druth Army, with an honorary commission of Lieutenant, of course she took it. What else was she going to do?

Six months into this morale tour, she was ready to do anything else.

The introductions continued in rapid fire, each lady taking position at center stage, so the audience could get a good look at them as they demonstrated their initial skills with their weapons.

Captain Olmen called out their name, their weapon, what archduchy of the nation they represented, and some bit of historical trivia that the audience could not give a single damn about.

And so it went: Delcoria Frain from Sauriya, expert swordswoman; Raxi Cresh from Patyma, master of the bow; Maxlynne Sunden of Kesta, pick; Volmay Keshin of Acora, axe; Theria Dare of Monim, hammer; Kelvanne Brownson of Oblune, pike; Chevren Loren of Yinara, trident; Evicka Renn of Linjar, chain flail; Argenitte Quire of Scaloi, mace.

It was absolute sewage, the whole idea. Fredelle was hardly a scholar of Druth military history, and even she knew the whole "traditional weapons of the archduchies" was nearly a complete fiction, threaded together from bits of lore and cultural identity that felt close to true. The use of most of these weapons in Druthal—especially their specialized use, the highly trained warriors—those were the old Elite Orders, now nearly all disbanded or folded into the military.

It didn't matter. This was a show. They knew their roles and performed as ordered. Fredelle would get through it. This one, then two more, and then back to Maradaine for a new assignment. She could bear it that long.

After the introductions, there were the series of showcases—solo performances or paired spars where the "fight" was perfectly choreographed. Some of the ladies would have costume changes for theirs, but Fredelle didn't bother. She wasn't trying to do anything more than her job, showing her skill with the staff. Plus, her scene was the second showcase, after Kelvanne and Evicka had their spar.

Fredelle always liked watching that one from the sidelines as she prepared to go on. For one, of all the other ladies , they were the ones who were most skilled in their weapons. Part of that was, for them, the stories of heritage and tradition were completely true. Kelvanne had come from so many generations of Oblunic pikemen, she had lost track. And Evicka had learned how to fight with the chain from her mother and her mother's mother. Both of them had wanted to be soldiers, and both took this job because they had thought it was the best way for them to be able to serve.

Their spar had a bit of theater—at least, Evicka provided the theater—of rivalry between them. Evicka had been part of the Royal First Irregulars before Fredelle had even joined, and had done this bit with Argenitte's predecessor. That had made more sense, as the historic rivalry between Linjar and Scaloi was legendary. But Argenitte had wanted no part of it, so Evicka took it up with Kelvanne, and it made for a better show.

Even though it was just a choreographed spar, Fredelle had watched it every night and never once saw the artifice in it. It was the same fight every time, and Evicka's precision with her chain was something to behold, but it looked as real and brutal as any fight ever could.

"Come on, Kelly," Evicka said. "Even with that, long, long pike in your hands…you can't get close to me." The taunt was part of the show.

"You haven't been able to land a strike, either," Kelvanne responded, though she never had any playfulness in her voice.

"Time to change that," Evicka said, and whipped the chain past her, then pulled the flail head back as it caught on Kelvanne's jacket.

"You wouldn't dare," Kelvanne said, flipping her pike around and catching the front button of Evicka's jacket.

"You want to test me?"

"Don't you dare."

Then they both pulled, and the curtain dropped at the same time.

Their performance was promoted as a demonstration of their martial skill with their weapons, but it was crafted to give the audience a sense that just maybe their uniforms would come off, intentionally or by 'accident'.

That would never actually happen in a performance. Captain Olmen was very strict about that point, and Fredelle was perfectly happy following those orders. And from the way Kelvanne spoke every time she cleared the stage after their bit, she would want to do away with that element completely.

"Stupidest thing," she growled as she passed Fredelle.

"I'm saying, it's that or kill each other," Evicka said. "Now let's get a drink."

Fredelle frowned, the least they could do was stay sober until the show was done. She made a gesture to one of the other ladies to stop them. She couldn't do it herself; she was about to go on. Nor could Theria or Volmay. They were out in the crowd when the curtain came back up, asking which of the boys out there had the best throwing arm and giving them apples.

"Good evening, gentlemen," Fredelle said. "My colleagues have been distributing a few dozen apples to those of you who claim you can throw. And I'm just up here, with my quarterstaff, saying that you cannot hit me."

One of two things always happened immediately. The first—which was exactly what happened—was that some fool threw his apple right away, thinking she wasn't ready yet.

But she was ready the moment the curtain came up, and with a casual spin of her quarter-staff, she knocked that apple off to the side.

"As I was saying," she said, "You cannot hit me."

Then the second thing happened—it was actually a rare performance that both didn't. One of the other soldiers called out, "What do we win if we do hit you?"

"Well," she said, making a show of touching her collar and inspecting her uniform coat. This was her one concession to the teasing in her showcase. "I suppose if you manage to get my uniform dirty…you get to keep it."

That was all it took for the boys to start throwing in earnest. Pure chaos, no sense of taking a turn or wanting to give her, as they presumed, a fair shot.

But she had learned her craft in three years as an Initiate in the Tarian order, where this exercise was done with hard wooden balls, and thrown by folks who were much better at it.

Despite the strength and skill with which those

apples were thrown, not one got past Fredelle's whirling shield of her staff. She blocked and knocked each one well away from her, not a single bit of apple touching her. All the while, keeping her eye on the crowd, noting the fellow who had that last apple, holding onto it.

Always one, bless the fool.

His fellows had exhausted their supply, and he wound up and threw harder and faster than any of them.

Fredelle whirled in a spin and cracked her staff against it, like she was hitting a triple-jack in tetchball, sending it rocketing back at him, splattering him in the chest.

"As I said," she cackled. "Not one of you would touch me."

"Fine," that fellow said, pushing through the crowd. "I'll settle for *these* apples!" He grabbed hold of Theria across her body in far too crass a manner.

Kelvanne was already bounding out to the crowd, her pike in her hand, as if she was going to cleave this bastard cleanly in two. Fredelle jumped in front, blocking her path with the staff. Theria could handle herself; she didn't need Kelvanne jumping in with murder in her eyes.

Theria reached up and grabbed the soldier's

head, and then dropped her weight while pulling him down, flipping him over her head. He landed flat on his back, and Theria was already back on her feet with her foot on his neck.

"Now, now," she said. "The show has rules, son, and you'd best follow them, hear?"

He just gurgled on the ground.

"We don't want nothing to ruin anyone's good time, right? So keep those hands to yourself."

She walked off, back behind the stage.

"Like I said," Fredelle said, pointing her staff at the crowd. "None of you can touch me. On with the show."

THE SHOW ENDED AS IT USUALLY DID: WITH minimal additional incident and a crowd of soldiers worked up to near frenzy. They were then told to disperse back to quarters, excited but vaguely disappointed.

Strictly speaking, they were delivered exactly what they were promised: a dazzling performance of martial skill and physical excellence by the Royal First Irregulars. They had not been promised a bird show—which neither the Crown nor the High Stars of the Druth Army would have approved of. That was explicit, that this be a show which reflected the morals and character of the Druth Army and the Crown and the good folk of Druthal. Therefore, while the boots on the ground might have wanted the bird show, it would never be one.

Even if there were a few ladies in the RFI who would have been happy to make it one.

Captain Olmen's job here as their commander was to act as chaperone and supervisor of morality. Fredelle had heard that she had been a cloistress before being made an officer to command the RFI. Olmen also acted as manager and producer for this tour; she did a lot of work. But she also was allowed to wear a normal uniform when she stepped out on stage.

After most shows, Fredelle preferred to walk it off, hiking around the grounds of whatever fort or outpost they found themselves at. The captain frowned at this but never said no. She may have been their chaperone, but she also knew her charges were ten adult women who could handle themselves.

Fort Mendallin was much like the other forts and outposts around northern Druthal—wood and stone, high walls, and aging battlements. And like most of these army bases up here, it was a relic, a posting that gave soldiers nothing to do. As much as she was frustrated with her role in the Royal First, at least she was doing something. The fellows of Fort Mendallin and the other placements in the Archduchy of Patyma would almost certainly never be called to action. At this point, the odds that there would be some sort of incursion from across the Gulf of Waisholm were incredibly low. The only reason there were soldiers placed here at all was politics, that every region and barony in the country wanted some form of garrison in place, just in case.

Bored soldiers were a problem, even a danger. Thus the "morale tour" of the Royal First.

It wasn't quite the chill of winter, but the night was crisp and cold with a strong wind. Fredelle had put a heavy fog coat on over her uniform, and the wind still cut through to her bones. She walked the interior of the perimeter, giving a nod to the boys who were on duty up in the battlements, who gave sleepy salutes back to her.

She was a lieutenant, after all, and she outranked them. While she had heard upper officers grumble about giving commissions to the ladies of the RFI , it served a purpose. Even as riled up as these boys got from their show, most of them knew damn well the consequence of crossing someone with stripes on their shoulders. That fellow who got too fresh with Theria was uncommon for these shows, and it was handled. Odds were that fellow would find himself with the worst duties on base for a month.

Fredelle approached the fort's officer club, which was little more than a cabin with better beer and tables than the barracks, and fires and lamps made it warm and inviting in the winter chill. Fredelle rarely availed herself of its comforts, but as she heard voices from inside, she could tell some of the other ladies were.

She stepped up to the door to see exactly who she expected. Maxlynne was sitting at a table with four officers, pouring from a bottle of Fuergan clear that one of them had broken out, cackling over some joke that she just made. Chevren was in the back corner, aggressively kissing some young man. And, of course, Raxi was making a spectacle of herself.

"Raxi," Fredelle said as she stepped in the doorway. "What are you doing?

Raxi had her bow drawn and a very sharp arrow nocked, aimed at a young soldier holding out his beer mug with the handle out. She gave a bleary eyed frown at Fredelle.

"I'm showing them this isn't some trick," she slurred. "That I really am that good a shooter— that I shoot that —that I am that good of a shot."

"She is that good," Fredelle said. "But if she's as in her cups as I think, well…" She shrugged. "Odds are, she'll still make that shot, actually."

"Like I said," Raxi said, glancing back at the man. "Now hold still."

"Shoot!" Maxlynne yelled.

"Please don't," Fredelle said.

"Freddie," Raxi said, her normally refined Patymic accent devolving more into a north hills country girl with each slurred word she drawled. "You've got to learn to relax and let loose, because you are just a tea kettle bubbling over with the whistle plugged."

"She hasn't been unplugged all tour!" Maxlynne said.

"Don't you worry about my…kettle," Fredelle said.

Raxi kept her gaze on Fredelle and winked. "And don't you worry about my aim." With that she let the arrow fly, and with a whooshing thud, the mug was torn out of the man's hand and pinned to the wall by the handle.

"I never do," Fredelle said. "But try to remember we're off for Watchpost Ten at first light, and you all need to be in a condition to make twenty miles tomorrow."

Chevren came up for air for the first time since Fredelle had been there, glancing at her. "Don't you know, we're never the ones you have to worry about. Stop slaughtering our fun." Without waiting for response, she dove back onto the officer's face.

"Who said I worry?" she asked, but she always did. And she knew the one she worried about the most wouldn't be in here. With a wave, she moved on toward the show space.

Their performance space was a temporary stage with simple curtain rigging and focused oil lamps, and a series of pitched tents that made up their backstage and camp on the fort's grounds. It was also designed—and Fredelle deeply admired the ingenuity of it—to be packed up and transformed into their wagons for heading to the next performance.

At this point, they could put up and strike it all in their sleep. In terms of duty, they weren't expected to do it until the morning before they headed out. But several of the women preferred to get part of the pack up settled before they went to sleep. Volmay and Theria were taking down the curtain and lamp rigging, while Evicka was nominally transforming the stage back into the wagons.

Nominally, because more of her attention was on sniping at the handful of enlisted soldiers who were still lurking around.

"Listen, you got to know Gonty didn't mean nothing by that," one soldier said.

"Oh, he didn't mean nothing," Evicka said. "You hear that, Theria? Groping you meant nothing."

"I know I've got more than nothing," Theria said.

"You can't hold it on him," another said. "You gotta tell the captain it was just good fun, let it go."

"Good fun?" Evicka asked, stepping away from the stage. "Hows about I slam a boot in your tenders, is that good fun?"

"That ain't—"

"Your boy assaulted an officer," Evicka said.

"Not a real one."

That got Volmay to drop down from the rigging and stalk over. "Not a what?"

"Not a—"

"What's on that shoulder, soldier?" she asked, pointing to her lieutenant's stripes.

"Yeah but—"

Theria was with them, the three women now standing like a wall.

"You mean 'yeah but, *sir*.'"

"I ain't calling you 'sir'!"

"Then 'Lieutenant,'" Evicka said.

"For show, it's a game!" one of the other boys said. That triggered a response in Evicka—one that Theria and Volmay would sure back up—that Fredelle knew she should stop. She stepped forward and roared out with her most commanding voice.

"We are commissioned officers in the Army of His Majesty, King Maradaine the Eighteenth, Sovereign of Druthal, and we are as sworn and signed to our duty as any other!"

That, at least, startled the enlisted men, as well as Theria and Volmay, who gently pulled Evicka back. She twisted her shoulder out of their grip, but didn't advance further on the soldiers.

"You can't have real charges on Gonty!" one of them said.

"He did real trouble," Evicka said. "He gets real charges."

"But you can't—"

"It's done, boys," Fredelle said, stepping forward. "I would suggest you get to your barracks, but instead, I'm going to order you to run a training around the course before you turn in. Maybe that will cool you all down a bit."

"You can't—"

"Should I tell your captain that you all disobeyed a direct order?" she asked. "If you're so keen to keep Gonty company."

They all scattered.

"We could have minced them," Evicka said.

"Of course you could have," Fredelle said. "But you rutting shouldn't."

"You going to help us with the breakdown?" Volmay asked, climbing back up on the rigging to take down the lamps. "Or you going to be wilding with the trio?"

"Not doing that, but I did check in on them," Fredelle said. "Just trying to keep you all out of trouble."

"I've got a mother and a captain," Theria said. "I don't need you, too."

"All right," Fredelle said.

Evicka was still stewing. "We *should* have minced them."

"Maybe you want to walk it off, too?"

"You can't order me."

"It's just a suggestion. But a good one."

Evicka shook her head. "I'll set the wagons for the morning."

"Fine. You seen Kelvanne?"

"You worried she's getting into trouble?" Evicka asked.

"Always." More often than not, Kelvanne was the one causing trouble. If Evicka was already this riled, Kelvanne must be fuming.

"I think she was backstage, packing with the Saints," Evicka said.

"Got it," Fredelle said, heading into the tents.

With any group spending too much time in close quarters together, smaller groups formed, and names for the other groups emerged. That had been the case in Fredelle's cohort in the Tarian Order, as well as her preparatory schooling before that. She was used to it. So Raxi, Maxlynne and Chevren were the Trio, which was really the Wild Trio. Theria and Volmay —easily the strongest of the ladies—were the Bruisers. Kelvanne and Evicka were the Brawlers, given they were the angry ones usually trying to start a fight. And Delcoria and Argenitte were the Saints, the ones who caused no trouble, did the most packing and cleaning, and took care of the details that should have been on everyone's shoulders.

Argenitte was also the one who spent her spare time with her nose in *The Testaments of the Saints*, made use of every chapel in every location they stopped in, and never held her tongue when she felt the others were behaving in an immoral manner.

"Is Miss Renn trying to fight a whole squadron?" Argenitte asked as Fredelle came in. She and Delcoria were loading up the trunks with all their performance material.

"It's handled," Fredelle said.

"You're still in your show uniform," Delcoria said quietly as she put a neatly pressed and folded outfit into the trunk.

"Sorry, I—"

"Were taking a walk, yes," Delcoria said. "It's a familiar routine."

Fredelle took off the coat and went behind the screen—the only one not packed away, so clearly they were waiting for her—and started to undress. "It's probably too late in the tour to break this routine."

"We all have our ways," Argenitte said. "Yours are far from worrisome."

"Hmm," Delcoria said.

Fredelle had never had a very long conversation with either of them, and the two of them, while usually in each other's company, seemed to mostly enjoy each other's silence. There were several rumors about them. That Argenitte was engaged to be married when she returned to Iscala, to a man she hadn't even met yet because her family had put it together. But there was also the rumor that she had committed some heinous sin, and serving in the RFI was her penance from the church. The stories about Delcoria were that she was already married, that her husband was a soldier who lost his legs, or that he owed a debt to the Kyst Bosses who broke his legs, and she was working to pay it off.

Fredelle didn't know if any of that was true, or any of the other stories about the other ladies. They all had a story; they all had some twisted reason to be here.

Fredelle's was simple: washed out of the Tarians, looking to do something, anything, that used her skills.

She came out from the screen in her chemise and skivs, handing the show uniform to Delcoria.

"A bid of modesty, Miss Pence," Argenitte said.

"I'm almost as covered as I am in that uniform," she said back. "Besides, my travel uniform seems to have vanished."

"I laundered it and hung it in the camp tent," Delcoria said, handing the coat back to Fredelle. "For the chill."

"Thanks," Fredelle said, putting it on. "They said Kelvanne was this way?"

"She came through here," Argenitte said tightly. "Her…familiar routine."

"I think she also went to the camp tents," Delcoria added with a hint more kindness in her tone.

Fredelle nodded and went out the back to their camp. She didn't even have to make it to the tents. Kelvanne was sitting on the cold ground, her pike in one hand and an empty bottle in the other.

CHAPTER TWO

"SO HOW DRUNK ARE YOU?"

Kelvanne didn't look up. "Seven generations. Seven generations of pikemen in the Druth Army. And before that, Brownsons held the pike for Lords of Oblune. And before that, we stood as Masters of the Braighian Order. My line—"

"So you're monologue drunk," Fredelle said. "Wonderful."

"And my father had only a daughter, but still he did his duty to me. Put a pike in my hands as an infant."

"All right, get up," Fredelle said, reaching out to take Kelvanne's hand.

"I am a soldier," Kelvanne said, pushing the offered hand away. "I was supposed to be. Instead…"

This was nothing new. After nearly every performance, Kelvanne got some form of blind drunk. There was brawling drunk, there was war stories drunk, and there was self-pitying monologue drunk, which was usually the last stage before passed-out drunk.

"Come on," Fredelle said, taking her by the shoulder and pulling her to her feet.

"Most of the rest of the girls don't get it. The show, the attention, the salary," She looked up at Fredelle, meeting her eyes. Kelvanne let the bottle drop—even as her grip on the pike remained firm—and cupped the side of Fredelle's face with her free hand. "But you understand, don't you? What we are, what we should be?"

"Kel, not—"

They were clearly at the phase that occasionally appeared between monologue drunk and passed-out drunk. Kelvanne pulled herself closer to Fredelle and kissed her, hard and rough and hungry.

"No," Fredelle said, pushing her back. "Not when you're drunk, never when you're drunk."

"That adds up to never, you know."

"I'll live with that," Fredelle said. "Let's get you to your bunk."

"That's what I'm talking about.," Kelvanne

said, opening up Fredelle's coat. "You're already ready."

Despite the charge Fredelle felt when Kelvanne's hand touched her bare skin, she took her wrist and pulled her hand away.

"You're going to sleep this off, Kel," Fredelle said. "Don't make me have to hurt you."

"You're the one who could," Kelvanne said. "Well, and Evicka, but she..." She trailed off. The passed out phase was coming.

"Let's get you in there before the captain sees either of us."

She half-carried Kelvanne into the tents, put her on her bunk, and took off her boots.

"You get it, though," Kelvanne mumbled. "You and Evicka, because you both understand what it really means to have to fight. What being a soldier, a warrior, is supposed to be. How we should be seen."

"All right, sleep," Fredelle said. "You'll feel worse in the morning."

"Always do, but I keep fighting."

"Two more stops, two more shows, and we're done."

"The saddest part," she said, her eyes closed now, "is this whole thing is *almost* a good idea.

We should be seen, we should be able to show them all how capable we are."

"We do, in this…twisted, carnival way," Fredelle said.

"Right," Kelvanne said. "But we need to be seen…as good at this as we actually are. Not 'as good as real soldiers.' We are real soldiers, and we should get to be."

"I'd rather we didn't need real soldiers," Fredelle said, "but some folks need good people to fight for them. That's why I wanted to be in the Order, and this…this is…"

Kelvanne's snoring interrupted that thought, and it was probably for the better.

Fredelle went and found her slacks and shirt, putting them on. She didn't know what secret Delcoria had for making them hang so crisply, but whatever it was, she did admire it.

"Fred?"

She looked up and saw Evicka in the tent entrance.

"What's going on?"

"It's the captain," Evicka said. "She's in a bad way, and she's asking for you."

THE FORT'S INFIRMARY WAS IN A PROPER building, and Fredelle had a brief thought about how odd it was that they were forced to camp within the fort's grounds instead of being given some form of officer's quarters—but that had been the arrangement the whole tour.

Two medics—the Yellowshield logo on the shoulders of their army uniforms—were on either side of a bed where Captain Olmen was attempting to sit up, looking an absolute fright. She had been stripped to her chemise and skivs, which were soaked with sweat and stained with vomit and blood, as was the bed. As Fredelle came in, Captain Olmen was emptying the contents of her stomach into a basin one of the medics was holding, while the other did his best to keep her upright.

"What happened?" Fredelle asked.

"Fever, vomiting, bleeding from…multiple orifices," one medic said as he helped her lie back down.

"But she was fine a couple hours ago."

"Lieutenant," Olmen wheezed.

"I don't think she was," the medic said. "She told us she's been having these symptoms, to a lesser degree, for some time now."

"What?" Fredelle asked. "What's wrong with her?"

"I'm at a loss," the medic said. "Have you or any of the other ladies had any symptoms?"

"Not that I'm aware of, but I wasn't aware of hers."

"Thought I…thought I…" Olmen said before bolting up again vomiting again.

"I can't rule out anything at this point," the medic said. "I'd like to have a quick look at you and the rest of the Royal First, in case there's some sort of infectious plague you've all been exposed to."

"Of course," Fredelle said. She turned to Evicka, still hanging in the doorway of the infirmary. "Let the rest know, gather them up in the tents. Spoil whatever fun they're having."

"And Kelly?" Evicka asked.

"She's already in the tents, not likely to go anywhere," Fredelle said.

Evicka looked past Fredelle to Captain Olmen. "Are those the orders, Captain?"

"Do…do what…Pence…says," Olmen said.

"Aye," Evicka said with a salute and went off.

"If not some form of plague, what else could it be?"

"I wouldn't rule out poison. She said she'd

been taking a tonic of chanaric mushroom to miti-gate her symptoms. Too much may have caused a bad reaction."

"Been…sick…for weeks…thought I could finish…tour."

"There's a rigidity to her belly," the medic said. "It's possible she has an invasive growth in her gut, which is the real source."

"How can you be sure?"

"I'm not inclined to cut her open unless we have to, and we don't have a surgeon here on the base. Maybe Yensic Falls, that's the closest town sizable enough; there's someone who could help her."

"Wrong…direction," Olmen said.

"It's your call on that, medic," Fredelle said.

"No. Tour continues."

"Ma'am," Fredelle said. "You're clearly in no condition."

"Keep…the schedule…lieutenant."

"What's your schedule?" the medic asked.

"Leave in the morning, three days travel to Watchpost Ten, then another three days to Fort Nanderack."

"And rough country at that," the medic said. "Even if the rest of you are clear of infection and I can allow you to leave, there's no way she can make that journey. I wouldn't even feel good about taking her to Yensic. I don't think she could survive any travel."

"Tour…schedule."

"Ma'am, you can't," Fredelle said to her. As if the captain's body wanted to prove the point, she began vomiting again, with a fresh release of blood coming from underneath her. "It's done."

"You can continue," Captain Olmen said. "Last two shows, then to Maradaine."

"Without you?" Fredelle asked.

"You, Lieutenant Pence. You command it."

"Ma'am, I'm not sure…"

"Those are your orders," Olmen said. "Do it, and I'll stay here."

"Aye," Fredelle said. "Orders received, ma'am."

Captain Olmen closed her eyes and lay back, while the other medic went to work pouring a tonic down her throat.

"You want to check me out, Medic?" Fredelle asked. "Then we'll go to the rest and see if we're cleared for travel, all right?"

He nodded and started to examine her with rough efficiency, fingers prodding her mouth and face before working their way down her body. She knew there was nothing wrong with her, or likely the rest of the Royal First, and the sooner he con-firmed it, the better.

She would need him as witness to Captain Olmen's orders, as well. Odds were strong the rest of the ladies wouldn't be too keen to accept Fredelle's command just on her say-so.

***

"YOU MUST BE KIDDING," CHEVREN SAID, glaring at Fredelle while she opened up her uni-form for the medic to examine her chest. "You're in command?"

"That's what Captain Olmen said."

"She did ask for Freddy," Evicka said. "And she told me to listen to her."

"I want to hear it from her," Delcoria said.

"I don't know if that's possible," the medic said as he finished with Chevren. "She's now lost consciousness, and I'm not inclined to wake her and force further strain on her."

"But continue without her?" Argenitte asked. "Is that wise?'

"I think it's capital," Kelvanne said from her bunk. Fredelle didn't even realize she was awake. "If we have to continue this blazing sewage, at least it'll be without her pushing us to be sweet and kind every step."

"We should be those things," Raxi said.

"Eat my belt, Raxi," Kelvanne snarled.

"Easy, easy," Fredelle said. "Look, I didn't ask for this, but it's what the captain said. Right, Medic?"

"I did hear that," he confirmed.

"So it's my command until we get further orders from someone higher up. The captain could barely speak, but she used what few words she had to insist we keep to the schedule."

"Those poor boys at Watchpost Ten need us," Volmay said with a cackle. "What would they do without us?"

"Have to stroke on each other," Maxlynne said with a snort.

"They'll have to do that anyway," Theria said. "Just they get to think about us when they do."

"Don't be crude," Argenitte said. She was submitting herself to the medic's examination now, but from behind a screen.

"So we do it, right?" Raxi asked.

"It's not up to a vote," Fredelle said. "We have orders. That's clear."

"Right, orders," Evicka said. "Very important, being good soldiers here."

"We are good soldiers," Kelvanne said, still lying down with her eyes closed.

"We're packing up and marching at dawn, presuming we're not quarantined here."

"I'm not seeing cause," the medic said. Pointing to Maxlynne, he said, "Other than I can't fathom how that one can stand up with so much whisky on her breath, you're all in fine health, no sign of any kind of plague."

"Please, even this drunk I could do my scene," Maxlynne said. "Where's my pick?"

"Packed away," Delcoria said. "With everything else."

"We're set except for these tents," Volmay said.

"Then we're off with the sunrise," Fredelle said. "So get some sleep, all, and we continue the tour."

"Finish the tour," Kelvanne mumbled.

Seeing a few frowning faces still—notably Theria and Evicka—Fredelle added. "Good. Last thing we need is any of us charged with insubordination. I'd hate to bring that to the fort's commanding officer."

"Right, lieutenant," Evicka said with a salute. "No problem here at all."

MORNING CAME TOO SOON IN FREDELLE'S opinion; she definitely had not slept enough. Not that she ever got much sleep after performance nights, but last night's crises had gone late and made sleep even harder to find. It was likely two bells after midnight when she finally lay in her bunk, and despite the fact they were this far north while approaching the winter nadir, it felt like the sun was already up moments after she put her head down.

Kelvanne was already dressed and packing, taking down the tents despite some of the ladies still sleeping under them.

"Rise it up," Fredelle said as she got her slacks on. "You don't need me to tell you your load out duties. I want to be on the road in half an hour."

It was true, the ladies knew their jobs, and all got to work as they got off their cots with a minimum of grumbling noises. Fredelle had her own usual duties for every load out, and despite her new responsibilities of command, she had no intention of shirking them or pawning them off on anyone else. Fundamentally, they were all still the same rank, with the same orders and assignment.

They should behave as if the captain was still coming with them.

But if the captain was coming with them, she would have been in charge of the maps and the route, and that was not something Fredelle specialized in. Sitting on the lead wagon while the others hitched up the mounts, she had rolled out the captain's map and was doing her best to figure out the route they needed to take. Captain Olmen's notes were chaotic and probably only made sense to her. Watchpost Ten was to the west, and they had two days of solid travel, if she was judging scale right.

"Kel," she said as Kelvanne was going past. "Can I borrow your eye?"

"What about it?" Kelvanne asked, coming over.

"Look at the map here," she said. "Am I right that we head out west from here, take this road through this mountain pass, camp at this point, then follow the road past this village, camp here second night, and then toward the coast for Watchpoint Ten by midday?"

"Route's fine," Kelvanne said. "I will point out the job is terrible, regardless, and given the situation, no one would blame us for not doing the last two shows."

"Last night you said—"

"Last night I was supporting you in front of the rest," Kelvanne said. "They needed to accept the captain gave you command. But I'm telling you, it's *your* command, and you can make whatever decision you want now."

"My orders are to finish the tour."

"Sure. But being an officer, in command, means you have to make a call on the field, and accept the consequences. So I got to ask you— what are the consequences to not finishing? Does anyone really care if we do or not?"

"I do, Kelvanne," she said sternly. "And you ought to as well."

Evicka had come over. "Finishing is a waste of time, though. You know all of this is beneath us." Leaning in, a little more conspiratorially, she added. "Especially *us.* " Her hand gestures indicated that she considered the three of them to be in a different class than the rest of the women in the Royal First.

"None of that, Evicka," Fredelle said.

"Look, your command," Evicka said, hands up in mock surrender. "I know who the best people here are, and there's a reason why the captain asked for you. She knew better than to put me or Kelly in charge."

"Well, I am in charge. Two more shows. You both can swallow your pride and handle it."

Evicka sighed and walked off, shaking her head.

"Fine," Kelvanne said. Her attention was back on the map. "Why take this route past the village? It looks like this ridge road would get us there in half the time. Give us more chance to rest before the show."

Fredelle looked at the map, where the captain had scribbled over the road and just written "NO" on the route Kelvanne pointed out.

"I'm guessing the captain knew something we don't about that route."

This time it was Maxlynne, coming to finish hitching the mounts to the lead wagon. "Which route?"

"The Golsin Ridge?" Kelvanne asked.

"Golsin?" Maxlynne furrowed her brow. "I heard the boys talk about there's a band of raiders who camp in those hills. Apparently the chaps in Watchpost Ten and Fort Nanderack are having a blazes of a time subduing them."

"So that's why the captain didn't want that," Fredelle said. "Makes sense to me."

"Band of raiders," Kelvanne said dismissively. "Shouldn't be an issue for us."

"Not worth the trouble. Coast road it is."

"We're ready to roll out," Maxlynne said. "Just give the word, ma'am."

"The word is given," she said. She raised her voice to issue a commanding call. "Royal First Irregulars! We're on the road!"

CHAPTER THREE

"ALL RIGHT, LADIES, LET'S GET set for camp. You know your duties, get on it!"

Most of the women got to work with their appointed tasks. They knew what they needed to do —prep the tents, fire for the dinner, secure their perimeter. They'd done it all dozens of times on this tour, no change now.

Except there was no Captain Olmen.

"Kel," Fredelle said. "Help me with the captain's camp tasks."

Kelvanne scowled, but nodded and came over to help Fredelle take the horses off their harness.

"Still a lot of daylight," Kelvanne said. "We should make another two miles."

"According to my map, we're in a fine place to stop and make our schedule," Fredelle said.

"Bad discipline," Kelvanne said. "We should

be going at a more controlled march, and we would be another two miles by now."

"I want to make camp and run a rehearsal before we bed down," Fredelle said. "And that means while we still have daylight."

"Rehearsal, are you serious?" Kelvanne asked, moving in close and aggressive.

Fredelle straightened her back, matching her eye to Kelvanne's. "I'm completely serious. We're giving a performance at Watchpoint Ten in two days."

"If we took the Golsin Ridge, we'd be there tomorrow."

"Orders said no."

"'No' was written on a map, not the same."

"*My* orders."

"Fred, that's—"

"You are always going on about how we need to be treated like real soldiers," Fredelle snapped. "Bad discipline, you just said. And yet you keep challenging my command."

Kelvanne looked like she had a retort to that but then bit her lip. "Yes, sir, you're right there."

"Damn right."

"We don't need to rehearse, though," Kelvanne said.

"Yes, we sh—"

Kelvanne got in absurdly close to Fredelle. "What we need to do is *drill*. Rehearsal is for actors. We are soldiers. We *drill*."

Blazes, she was right about that. Where had Fredelle picked up the word "rehearse"? In the Tarians, when she had been an Initiate, that was never the word. Train. Drill. Maybe practice.

Captain Olman. She had been the one to say it.

Fredelle parried and pivoted from Kelvanne's offensive. "What do you know about the captain? Her background?"

"Not much," Kelvanne said. "Not military, I'll tell you that."

"She grew up with a touring company of actors," Evicka said, coming up on them both. "Her whole childhood was spent going from town to town, putting on a new show in each place. Her and her mother were the ones who made sure the company ran like the clock in a church tower. Her mother died when she was in her adolescence, the company fell apart, and she went to RCM and studied arts and history. From there, she was recruited to be part of the king's 'Morale Corps' that we're all in, precisely because of her experience of running a traveling performance."

Fredelle and Kelvanne both stared at Evicka.

"How did you know all that?" Kelvanne asked.

"Because I'm a very good listener, and I remember everything about everyone," Evicka said. She gave them both a meaningful glance, adding, "I know *everyone's* secrets."

"Well, that explains how 'rehearsal' slipped into our vocabulary," Fredelle said, sidestepping Evicka's implication. "You're right, we should *drill* tonight, Kel."

"And march at soldier's pace tomorrow," Kelvanne said. "Am I right, Vick?"

"Not my call," Evicka said. "But she's probably right."

"No, in that, we'll keep the captain's method and pace," Fredelle said. "She may not have been a soldier, but she did know what she was doing as far as traveling and performing. And before you make another snap, *Lieutenant*, that is our mission. We're not marching to make best time for a fight. Our assignment in this army is the morale corps, and we give a performance. So, the right practice for the right job."

"Whatever you say, Acting Captain Pence," Kelvanne said with a salute. That touch of disrespect. Kelvanne wanted discipline, then Fredelle would give her discipline. But in a way that would also maintain peace for the duration. Extra duty, but one she wouldn't argue over.

"Also, you're to sergeant our drills for the rest of the tour. Understood?"

A hint of a smile found its way onto Kelvanne's face. "Yes, ma'am."

As FREDELLE HAD SUSPECTED, GIVING KELVANNE the responsibility of running the rehea—the drills, rather—cooled off her other complaints. The evening went smoothly, though Kelvanne's run of the performance was intense. Fredelle suspected no one would have trouble falling asleep after that.

As an extra touch of discipline, she assigned Kelvanne the first watch of the night while the rest slept, and then the rest of the shifts, taking the final one just before dawn for herself. That was how she liked it, anyway—an uninterrupted night, and an early rise while the world was quiet to see the sunrise. She was ready for another day on the road when Chevren woke her for her shift.

Having that dawn light to herself was a blessing. She did not expect any trouble, they only had a watch as a precaution, and on the whole tour the most excitement any watch shift had was the night Raxi saw a pair of foxes. So she took her quarterstaff, stepped into the road away from the rest of the camp, and ran her own drills.

The Tarian Order was known for training in defensive fighting techniques, using shields in every way possible. But the quarterstaff training was just as integral. Centuries ago, there had been the Kenalian Order, nimble warriors trained to make use of minimal resources: no armor, no weapons but a wooden stick. When they disbanded, the remaining members—and their skills and techniques—were folded into the Tarians. There had once been a dozen different orders in Druthal, each with their own styles and techniques. To a large degree, that was the real origin of the "weapon from each Archduchy" nonsense their show promoted. The quarterstaff techniques she was drilling through, that came from the Kenalians, nothing to do with the Archduchy of Maradaine.

Just like Argenitte's mace and Evicka's flail came from the Otajian Order, Chevren's trident from the Marenian Order, Kelvanne's pike from the Braighian Order. But that was ancient history, all of the old orders had disbanded except the

Tarians and Spathians—and those were likely to shutter in her lifetime. No one wanted to hear about that, not when they were trying to promote the idea of a united Druth military.

That was her job: promote the idea of the Druth Army, make enlisting look like an attractive choice, and keep the fellows who made that choice happy. So she would twirl her staff in impressive-looking ways, and wear a "uniform" that made a schoolgirl skirt look reserved, and do her duty as ordered.

But in this moment, she was again working her weapon like she was trained, going through her sequences, and to have that in the peaceful quiet of the dawn was blissful.

"Morning," Kelvanne said, walking up with her pike slung over her shoulder. "Those are some proper moves."

"How long have you been up?"

"Enough to see something troubling on the horizon," Kelvanne said.

Fredelle looked up. "Doesn't seem like a storm is coming."

"Not weather," Kelvanne said. "Come up on the ridge over here."

Fredelle followed her up a rough trail off the road to the top of a small cliff, from which they had a spectacular view of the valley extending beyond them.

"There's our road to Watchpost Ten," Kelvanne said, pointing along one way. "Road splits off there, leading to that village in about a mile, and then beyond to further north."

"All right, and?"

"And, just a bit to the east, in that clearing," Kelvanne said, handing Fredelle a lensescope.

Fredelle looked through the scope.

A group of men—at least two dozen, maybe more—were packing up a camp. Men with horses and swords. And not men in any kind of uniform.

"Those raiders we heard about?" Fredelle asked.

"I would think so."

Fredelle took that in. "They're pretty far from our road. I doubt it'll be an issue."

Kelvanne scoffed. "Look at them again. They're checking their weapons, wearing lined coats. They're putting barding on their horses. They're getting ready for a fight."

"So we march hard, we should get ahead. Good eye on this."

Fredelle started back down to the camp.

"You idiot!" Kelvanne shouted after her. "They aren't getting ready to fight us. They don't even know we're up here. They're getting ready to attack that village!"

———

"WHO'S AN IDIOT, WHAT?" RAXI ASKED, COMING up the trail. The rest of the ladies were all awake now, striking their tents, getting the wagons ready.

"No one, let's ease up," Fredelle said. "We've got a bit of an issue, but we can handle it."

"Bit of an issue?" Kelvanne snapped. She stormed past Fredelle, charging toward her tent.

"Watch it, Kel!" Delcoria shouted at her. "Stomping around with your weapon, you could hurt someone!"

"That is the point of it!" Kelvanne snapped back. "This pike was held on the beaches of Falsham! Generations of Brownsons held the pike and fought for their lives, for the lives of their countrymen! That is what it's for! Not to be spun around in a show for morons!"

"Is she drunk already?" Volmay asked.

"I don't think so," Fredelle said. "She just needs to cool down."

"It's too early for this sewage, Kelly," Evicka said.

"No, this is the sewage," Kelvanne said. "Right now, down in that valley, a village is about to get attacked."

"A what?" Maxlynne asked.

"Go up on that ridge, you'll see!" Kelvanne shouted. "Won't they, Lieutenant Pence?"

Eight sets of eyes focused on Fredelle. "There's a group of armed men breaking camp, in galloping distance of the village."

"So they're going to attack the village?" Argenitte asked.

"I can't speak for their intentions," Fredelle said. "And neither can Kelvanne."

"They're armed men, armoring their horses," Kelvanne said. "We have a duty to defend that village."

"We have a what?" Maxlynne asked.

"Are you going to respond that way to everything?" Theria asked. "Armed and armoring? What sort of outfits?"

"Ragtag, disorganized," Kelvanne said.

"And how many?" Volmay asked. "What are we calling a group?"

"That's not our job," Argenitte said.

"What isn't our job?" Evicka asked. "I thought we were soldiers."

"This isn't a war, this is a…local skirmish."

"Two dozen armed men about to thunder on a mining village is a skirmish?" Kelvanne asked.

"Two dozen?" Volmay asked.

"At least," Fredelle said. It was absurd. There was no way the ten of them should do this. Most of them may have had training in their weapons, fulfilled the requirements to nominally earn their rank, but many of them had never been in real combat before. Raxi had been a trickshot archer in a carnival. She could hit a target shooting with her feet, but there was no way she was equipped for this.

But yet, this part of her heart knew that Kelvanne was *right*. More than that, in a dark way, she wanted to get into a fight herself.

"Twenty-four armed men, with horses?" Theria asked. "We wouldn't stand a chance."

"And that village would?" Delcoria offered.

"Are you seriously saying we should join in this fight?" Maxlynne asked.

"No. I'm saying we must. That we have a *duty* to." Kelvanne shook her head and put on her heavy padded coat. "At least I do. If that means I go alone, so be it."

"You won't go alone," Evicka said.

"Stop it," Fredelle said. "No one is going off alone."

"Are you going to stop me?" Kelvanne asked. Her grip on her pike tightened, like she was eager for a starter course.

"No," Fredelle said. She hated that Kelvanne had made this a confrontation, but, damn her, she was right. "But we cannot go in like mad boars, either."

"So we're going in?" Chevren asked.

"If innocent people will be hurt, and we do nothing to stop it, the sin would fall upon us," Argenitte said. "Acting is a moral imperative."

"First Irregulars!" Fredelle called out. If she was in command, she would do it properly. "Ready three of the horses for riding, two riders per horse. Heavy coats, weapons ready. Theria and Volmay, Delcoria and Argenitte, Chevren and Evicka. Be ready to ride down to the village road and prepare for engagement on the outskirts. Raxi, Maxlynne, hitch all wagons to the remaining horse, take it down to the road junction and be prepared for retreat, treating the wounded. If you deem it necessary to flee, ditch the wagons and go at gallop speed to Watchpost Ten."

"And you and Kelly?" Evicka asked.

"We're scouting ahead on foot straight away. You've got your orders, Irregulars. Move on them."

CHAPTER FOUR

"SLOW DOWN," FREDELLE URGED KELVANNE as caught up to her. Kelvanne had all but broken into a sprint, bounding down the path to the main road.

"Can't keep up?"

"It's not about keeping up," Fredelle said. "If we have a fight on our hands when we get there, I don't want you already worn out."

"Worry about yourself," Kelvanne said.

Fredelle wasn't worried about that. Long-distance running was a key part of conditioning for the Tarian Initiates. By her third year, she could run the entire city east to west and north to south and still go through her drills. "Just keep pace with me, all right?"

"Those raiders could already be on the village now."

"Maybe," Fredelle said. "We don't really have a plan if it comes to a fight."

"I'm partial to 'carve them up with a pike,' myself."

"Think, Kel," she said as they reached the junction. This was where Raxi and Maxlynne should wait with the wagon, their point of escape if they needed it. The main road west to Watchpost Ten, and the narrow one into the woods, to the village. "Take a breath."

"Those folks in that village won't be able to."

"Give me a moment to think of something resembling a strategy here."

"If we're lucky, they haven't already reached the village," Kelvanne said, pacing in the junction.

"Best case," Fredelle said. "We get there ahead of them, or before they really start any chaos, and our mere presence as imposing women in uniform sends them running."

"That won't happen."

"Let me dream."

"Dream and move," Kelvanne said, heading down the road. "You wanted the two of us to go ahead for a reason."

"Four horses, ten ladies," Fredelle said. "Best math is still two on foot."

"And we're the ones best suited for a fight," Kelvanne said.

Fredelle wasn't sure about that. She had been trained for it, but Kelvanne…someone she wondered if Kelvanne just wanted the fight. She was gifted with the pike, but that meant something else when it was a real fight against someone trying to kill you. In that skirmish at the party back in Maradaine, Kel had gotten pretty badly hurt. She had almost been replaced in the Royal First.

"Our real best hope is getting ahead of these raiders, using our reach to push them back, and having the rest of the squadron come up behind, box them in."

"So we're not waiting for the others to catch up," Kelvanne said. It wasn't a question.

The village was maybe still a half mile off, but they could already hear that they were not getting there ahead of the raiders.

"We don't have the luxury," Fredelle said. "Best plan is move fast, hit hard, cause pain."

"I like that plan."

"Kel," Fredelle urged. "I mean pain. We can't fight two dozen men, but if we really hurt three or four, the rest might rethink the value of a fight. Get them to bolt. That's the best chance we have."

They emerged from the woods, into a

clearing and the first houses of the village. A few of the raiders were dragging folks out of their houses, smoke pouring out the windows. More of them could be seen riding through the village square.

"Oh, I can make them hurt, all right," Kelvanne said. Holding her pike high, she broke into a sprint.

There was nothing more for Fredelle to do but run with her, deep into the fray.

———————————————

FREDELLE HAD ONLY SUBDUED ONE RAIDER—cracking her staff across his knee to send him to the ground, and then pinning his fighting arm behind his back and yanking it until it made a sickening pop—when she lost sight of Kelvanne. They should have stayed together, had each other's backs, but instead Kel was deep in the smoke and the shouting.

Fredelle's raider was on the ground, screaming in agony, which was exactly what Fredelle wanted from him. A message to his compatriots. He wasn't going to stand up or use that arm again today, but she knocked his sword away from him just the same. He had a knife in his belt, and she took that as well.

"Are you all right?" she asked the village woman he had been dragging out of her home. "Are you hurt?"

"No," the woman answered, and without further clarity, Fredelle presumed that was the answer to both questions.

"Anyone still inside?"

"I'm gonna rip out your guts!" the man on the ground shouted between his screams. Fredelle answered that with a boot in his face.

"My husband, he's hurt," the woman said.

Fredelle went into the house—smoke was pooling along the ceiling, but she could still see. The main source of the fire came from a wooden table, where an oil lamp had been knocked over. The woman's husband was half under the table, his skin turning red. The table was too engulfed for Fredelle to put it out, so she hooked her staff under the closest leg of the table and dragged it out the door.

"What are you doing?" the woman demanded.

"Saving your house and your husband," Fredelle said. She got the table far enough away that it couldn't make anything else catch fire and ran back in. Grabbing a blanket to beat out the remaining flames, she stopped the fire and got to the man on the ground. He was still breathing, as blood trickled from the gash in his head. Fredelle dragged him out by his legs into the fresh air.

"You got something to tie him up?" Fredelle asked the woman, as the raider was trying— poorly—to crawl over to his sword.

"Aye," the woman said, and she tossed some leather straps over to Fredelle while she knelt down to tend to her husband. Fredelle flipped the raider over on his stomach, strapped his arms to each other, and then bound his legs. This started a new round of screaming in agony.

Good.

Hoofbeats behind her. Shouting.

Fredelle spun around while whipping her staff into a fighting stance. Another one of the raiders was bearing down on her on his horse, sword high.

He clearly thought he was at the advantage on horseback. Against most folks, he would be. But Fredelle had reach, she had training, she had maneuverability. His horseback charge was almost wild, he went right past her, swinging his blade at empty air while she darted around. A wide swing of her staff knocked him off the horse and flat on his back. Gasping for air, he couldn't manage to cry out in pain as her next two swings disarmed him, then incapacitated him.

"You got him, too?" she asked the village woman.

"Aye," she said, rage in her voice. Fredelle nodded and ran after the horse. It was a perfectly good horse, after all. She was quickly able to grab hold of its rein, step into one stirrup with ease, and launch herself onto the saddle. Turning it toward the village, staff nestled in the crook of her arm like a lance, she spurred it to gallop into the fray.

There, in the village center, she saw Kelvanne. She had planted herself in front of the entrance to the public house, guarding the door. A mangy black-and-white dog had taken a position next to her, barking like mad at the raiders. At least six men tried to charge her as she spun her mighty blade so none of them could approach without being cut to shreds. One man was on the ground, his entrails in his hands as proof of her skill and conviction.

And the smile on her face, it was glorious.

Fredelle galloped into the fray, crashing her staff into one of the raiders, sending him back. As she turned back around for another pass, she saw the village square was now filled with more of the raiders, several on horseback, all of them with swords. At least twenty of them.

"Looks like some birds want to play soldier," one of them—a greasy-haired hulk of a man with a beard down to his belly—said with a tone that indicated he was the leader. "Get 'er off that."

One of his men—the only one with a bow— drew two arrows and fired at Fredelle. Or rather, her horse. It dropped, and she barely had a chance to dismount to avoid being crushed by it.

These bastards were more than willing to kill a horse.

"We don't just play," Kelvanne shouted. "Royal First Irregulars!"

"Eat that one up," he commanded his men, pointing to Kelvanne. Turning to Fredelle, he added, "I want her."

Sword out, he came hard at Fredelle. She was ready to parry and counter, but this fellow had skills. Not as easily dispatched as his compatriots. He grinned, and started to taunt her.

"I'm going to enjoy running you—" he was saying when Theria's hammer crashed into his head. Fredelle took the moment to take her own swing, cracking him across the chest.

He stumbled back, clearly in a daze as he

looked around, seeing the other ladies of the RFI coming in to mop up his men.

"Run out, boys!" he shouted as he shambled over to a horse that had lost its rider to Chevren's trident. "Get out of here!" Those raiders that could still run or ride did so with great haste, while the rest were quickly subdued by the rest of the RFI.

"You all right, boss?" Theria asked as she strolled over to get her hammer.

"On my feet, guts still inside me," Fredelle said. "Can't complain about that."

"No, ma'am," Theria said.

"We should run them down," Evicka said.

"No, we've got to deal with these prisoners," Delcoria said.

"And help the victims and survivors," Argenitte added.

"They're right," Fredelle said. But seeing that Evicka was still in a heaving state, whatever fighting lust she had not slaked, she added, "But go to the junction just in case those fellows come up on Raxi and Maxlynne. They shouldn't be alone."

"Aye," Evicka said, and she ran off.

"I could—" Kelvanne started.

"Stay right there, Kelly," Fredelle said. "You did damn good, but let's take a breath and have that looked at." She pointed to the gash in Kelvanne's side.

"Huh," Kelvanne said, looking down. "Now when did that happen?"

INJURIES AMONG THE ROYAL FIRST WERE MINIMAL —Kelvanne's slash on her side being the worst of them, and she insisted that was nothing to worry about.

The dog had not left her side.

"We should find that mutt's owners," Fredelle told her as she stitched up Kelvanne's wound.

"I think they're already dead," Kelvanne said. "I ran in, and two of those bastards had already carved a couple up, and one was kicking this boy right here." She reached out and scratched its ears, and it happily licked at her hand. "I made it very clear how unacceptable I found that."

Most of the villagers had managed to get into the public house Kelvanne had been guarding. Those that made it inside were largely fine, at least physically. Those that hadn't—

Those that hadn't, the one saving grace was

that the arrival of the Royal First Irregulars had prevented the raiders from engaging in any extended cruelty. People had been hurt, people had been killed—it had been a tragic day for this village, no doubt. But it could have been much worse.

So people were patched up. Fires were put out. Losses were mourned.

The raiders who had not been able to run away were bound, stripped of all weapons and locked away in one of their cellars. Folks ran for the archduchy sheriffs in the next town to deal with the prisoners, and the villagers assured Fredelle that they could handle things.

Evicka had returned with Maxlynne and Raxi and the wagons in tow. The ladies all got to work putting things back into their usual travel mode. By mid-afternoon, with the profound thanks of the villagers, they were ready to get back on track, though with an additional traveler.

"That dog coming with us?" Volmay asked Kelvanne as they were finalizing the packing up. Indeed, the black-and-white haired mutt had jumped into the back of one wagon, making his intention very clear.

"He's got no one else," Kelvanne said, petting the dog, still smiling like Fredelle had never seen from her before. "So it seems he's fixing himself to come with us."

"Did you ask who he should go to?" Fredelle asked.

"There was someone who was a cousin of the owners, but he said he never got along with the dog, and, well…he seems happy with us, yeah?"

"We're going to take him?" Delcoria asked.

"Why not?" Chevren asked, sitting next to the dog on the wagon. He responded by licking her face enthusiastically. "He seems a very good dog who needs good folks."

"If he is orphaned and we're not removing him from rightful owners, I see no moral reason not to have him join us," Argenitte offered.

Evicka frowned. "He's your all's problem, I'm not taking care of him."

Raxi looked at Fredelle. "What's the order on the dog, Lieutenant?"

"I think…we officially have the mascot of the Royal First Irregulars."

Kelvanne gave the dog a vigorous rub. "You hear that, buddy? You're one of us now."

That settled, the dog and the ten ladies of the Royal First Irregulars were back on the road to Watchpost Ten.

CHAPTER FIVE

NEWS OF THEIR BATTLE HAD managed to reach Watchpost Ten before the Irregulars did—and they arrived a day later than scheduled. The two soldiers at the gate had definitely heard about it, and were excited to get the details direct from the ladies as soon as they had arrived.

"How many were there?" the lead soldier asked.

"Heard one of you held off twenty of them!"

"Who told you that?" Fredelle asked, but Evicka jumped off the wagon and put herself in front of her.

"Now, now, we can't be giving everything away right here at the gate, lads, what sort of girls do you think we are? No, no, you want to know about our exploits, you need to come to the show!"

"Come on, ladies," the first soldier asked. "Give me a little."

"Like we haven't heard that before," Volmay said.

"Maybe Chevren will give him a little."

"Not right at the gate! He's gotta earn it!"

"Don't be vulgar, ladies."

"Too late!"

"Easy!"

"Chevren already is!"

"Ladies!" Fredelle barked. "A little decorum, hmm?" They had all been punchy, if not outright giddy, for the whole rest of the journey here.

"Sorry, ma'am," Theria offered.

"We're already behind schedule here, gents," Kelvanne said. "Can we get a move on?"

They opened the gate and let the wagons through, and were shown the spot in the courtyard to put up their stage.

"Lieutenant Pence?" a young officer asked as he came over. "The watch commander would like a word."

Fredelle gave orders for everyone to keep at it as she followed him to the commander's office.

The commander was a stern, austere looking

man who gave the impression of having never been acquainted with joy. He didn't even look up from the papers on his desk as she came in.

"You're in command of these…performers?" he asked.

"I've been assigned command in the absence of our captain," Fredelle said. "Though we're all lieutenants."

"So it's your fault you're late. Your performance was scheduled for last night."

"I'll take responsibility for that, yes, sir," Fredelle said. "We encountered a situation on the road that we had a moral imperative to attend to. It would have been a dereliction of duty to ignore it, and if I have to choose between that and tardiness, I choose tardiness every time."

"Hmmm," the commander grunted. "And yet reports of your exploits reached us before you did."

Fredelle knew when she was being baited, and she wasn't going to take it. Of course a runner from the villages, or the archduchy sheriff, or even Fort Mendallin could have beaten them here. A lone rider could do it in less than a day if they didn't care about the horse. She had ten soldiers and wagons filled with equipment, and had made good time, given the circumstances. This commander wanted her to defend herself, to give him excuses. But he wasn't the type to take excuses, even if he wanted to have one to tear into her further.

"I'm glad messengers were able to reach you efficiently," she said. "My people are setting up for our performance this evening, if that suits your needs, sir."

"The men need it," he said grimly. "No need to punish them for your sloppiness."

"I agree, sir."

"Seven bells then, punctually."

"We'll be ready, sir."

"Very well." He took one paper off his desk. "Also, Captain Olman, your commander, did not recover from her illness. When you return to Maradaine you'll want to have your office reach out to her people, if you don't feel a…moral imperative to do it yourself." He extended the paper to her.

"I appreciate the news, sir," she said, taking the report. "If there's nothing else?"

"Do your little show for the men, try not to rile them up, and be off my base by morning. Dismissed."

"Sir," she said with a salute and happily left his presence.

The ladies were well along in setting up the stage and the tents when she returned. "Irregulars," she called out. "Huddle around."

"What's the word, chief?" Volmay asked.

"First off, there's been word from Fort Mendallin. Captain Olmay succumbed to her illness."

"Oh, may the saints guide her," Delcoria said, as Argenitte went immediately into prayers.

"Do they know what her illness was?" Raxi asked. "Any chance that…I mean, we were all around her…"

"The doc over there said we were clean," Chevren said.

"Clean of what, unless we know what she was sick with."

"Cerulean fever takes weeks to show," Theria said. "Killed whole villages near where I grew up."

"Does anyone feel sick?" Maxlynne asked.

"We're fine, stop being trouble," Evicka said. "What else is there, boss?"

"We go ahead with tonight's show," she said. "The boys here 'need' it, apparently."

"I bet they do," Kelvanne muttered.

"So we do the show," Fredelle said. "But let's do the show *we* need, hmm?"

THE CHOREOGRAPHY DID NOT CHANGE. THAT WAS locked in, and none of the ladies wanted to mess with that and hurt themselves.

But they did change the costumes. Most of them, at least. Fredelle gave the order to dress as they felt most comfortable, as long as it reasonably looked like the uniform of the King's Army of Druthal. For most of them, that meant performing in their travel uniforms—long slacks and practical boots. Argenitte incorporated a hooded cloak, fully embracing a cloistress look. Chevren went in the other direction, not only wearing her show uniform, but undoing more of the buttons.

It was clear the fellows of Watchpost Ten liked Chevren's set the best.

The big change was in their speeches. Fredelle took the opening, in place of Captain Olmen—and asked for a prayer on the captain's behalf—and instead of the sewage and spin of the ten weapons of the ten regions, introduced each of the ladies as the women they actually were. Raxi learning trickshots at the circus, Chevren growing up on the docks of the Lacanja port. Kelvanne's heritage of Oblunic Pikemen, including her ancestors who served in the island war.

And when each lady took her time on stage, she told a story of her own. A story about the battle the other day. A story about picking up an axe as a child. A story about a fight in preparatory school.

A story about her training to be a Tarian.

The show was not as popular as their previous ones. Far less hooting and hollering. But the applause at the end, it had…respect.

And yet, at the end, Fredelle felt hollow about it. She couldn't quite figure out why—they got to do the show the way she wanted, and the boys of Watchpost Ten had enjoyed the show, but yet…

The other girls broke off after the show, mostly in the manner that they usually did. Raxi, Maxlynn and Chevren to the officers club. Volmay and Theria, Delcoria and Argenitte breaking down the stage and packing up the equipment. This time, Evicka went with the Trio, and Kelvanne—

Kelvanne was sober, playing with the dog.

And Fredelle realized what was lacking.

She went up to Kelvanne, absently scratching the dog's ears as she came in close.

"Aren't you usually doing your walk right now?" Kelvanne asked.

"Didn't seem right," Fredelle said, in a low whisper. "You know, I always tell you, never when you're drunk."

Understanding flashed in Kelvanne's eyes. "I'm not drunk now."

"I noticed that."

"We should get to the tents, then."

"I was thinking the same thing."

And that was that.

BY SOME MIRACLE, THEY WERE NOT INTERRUPTED in the tent, though Fredelle had a sneaking suspicion that someone—probably Delcoria—had spotted them and kept everyone else out to give them a few minutes. Whoever it was, they had Fredelle's blessings.

Kelvanne laid back down on the cot, letting out a satisfied sigh. "Saints, this is who we should be."

"I'm not sure exactly what you mean, but I don't disagree," Fredelle said with a light chuckle. She wanted to get up, find her skivs and uniform —whatever privacy they had been granted couldn't last too much longer—but also didn't want to move ever again.

"I mean, we got to be real soldiers, properly, even in the stupid show," Kelvanne said.

"This is what you were thinking about?" Fredelle asked. "I may have lost my touch."

"You absolutely did not," Kelvanne said. "I'm just thinking clearly for the first time in a while."

"Because you aren't drunk."

"Not wrong." Kelvanne turned so she was looking right at Fredelle, a gaze more focused and intense than she had ever seen from her. It felt more intimate and vulnerable than anything they had just done. "But I mean, being in that fight, helping those people, that's what it's all about, don't you think?"

"It felt really good, I'll admit." Fredelle said. "I mean, that's why I wanted to be a Tarian in the first place. To protect folks like that. Like I couldn't when…well, it doesn't matter."

"When what?"

Fredelle hadn't told this story to anyone, save the Tarian Master who interviewed her when she first applied for her Initiacy. "I grew up in Hertick Cove."

Kelvanne sat up at that. "Oh my saints, really?"

Fredelle knew that Kelvanne had been enough of a student of military history, especially the war with the Poasians, to know the significance of that town. One of the few battles of the war that didn't take place in the Napolic Islands. Part of the only successful incursion on the Druth mainland, late in the war.

"How old were you?" Kelvanne asked.

"Five," Fredelle said. The memory of it was mostly a blur of shouting, doors crashing open, her father being dragged—

She shuddered, realizing how much that raid had *felt* exactly like that.

"I read *The War Journals*," Kelvanne said. "It took three days for the soldiers from Fort Kordastin to reach the town. By that time, most folks had been…"

She didn't finish her sentence, probably because she knew damn well that Fredelle knew how it ended.

"Three days, where most of the kids and mothers were cowering away in root cellars."

"Most?"

"When the Poasians smashed into our house, they slaughtered my father, right there on the dirt. And they dragged my mother out into the garden when…this marvel of a woman, carrying a shield and a quarterstaff, she came at those ghosts and knocked them about like she had been sent by the saints. She told my mother to run, scooped me up in her arms, and hid us both in another house the Poasians had already torn through. Up in the attic, we hid, and she went back out there, to take on more of them. To save more people."

"Carilla Postarn," Kelvanne said. "A Tarian adept."

"You knew her name?" Fredelle asked.

"I've read all the journals, and her name…like Xandra Romaine, Tonia Illestin, Lady Quendina… they stayed with me. They told me that I could be the same soldier my father and his father and all the Brownsons before us could be."

"She was why I joined the Tarians, so I could be like her."

Kelvanne sighed. "I did try to join the Spathians, you know."

"I did not know."

"Didn't even get accepted as an Initiate. Was told I was too undisciplined."

"I don't think they were entirely wrong." Her one time in a training exercise with the Spathian Initiates was absurdly intense, even by Tarian standards.

"Even still, that's what I meant when I said

what we should be," Kelvanne said. "Not just that we should be saving villages or what have you. But that…instead of going around giving fancy skinshows to the boys in the encampments—"

"It's not a skinshow."

"It's worse, it's a skinshow that doesn't even have the decency to be honest that it's a skinshow."

Fredelle laughed. "Fair enough."

"Instead of, you know, 'inspiring' the boys, it's the girls in this country we need to inspire. Let them know that if they want, they could be like us."

Fredelle felt that in her heart. "Maybe we can convince our superiors to let us do exactly that."

"I think—"

Whatever Kelvanne thought, she didn't get to say, because Delcoria came into the tent, keeping a hand over her eyes.

"Pardon, Lieutenant Pence," she said. "I don't mean to disrupt whatever…meeting you're having in here."

"It's fine, Del, what's wrong?"

"There's some business happening in the officer club and our ladies there, they're asking for you to come sort it."

"Duty calls," Kelvanne said.

"The burdens of leadership," Fredelle said, getting out of the cot reluctantly, finding her clothes on the ground. "I'll be right there, Delcoria."

Delcoria scurried out of the tent.

"To be continued later?" she asked Kelvanne as she got dressed.

"For as long as we're on this road together, I certainly hope so," Kelvanne said. "I'll help pack, you sort out this business."

CHAPTER SIX

THE BUSINESS TURNED OUT TO have been Evicka, who was no longer at the officers club. Chevren, Maxlynne and Raxi were still there, and somehow they had ended up shackled by the base watch, as had several of the officers. There was a fair amount of blood on the floor, and it seemed the officers whose noses were bleeding had been the main source of that. Chevren had a busted lip as well.

"Are the shackles really necessary?" she asked the base commander, who had arrived at the same time she did.

"Standard procedure when the boys get to brawling in here," he said. "Then they sit in the brig for the night to cool."

"Not fair, chief," a soldier said. "That wild Linjari gal started things!"

"Is that true?" Fredelle asked her officers.

"I can't rightly say if she did or not," Maxlynne said. "Things started, she and I were sharing a bottle with these lads, and playing cards, while Rax and Chev were at the other table. Everything was going all pleasant-like, some new boy comes in joins us."

"And the Linnie went nuts!" a soldier cried.

"That ain't the truth of it," Maxlynne said. "Truth is, he sits down, and Vick, she gets up and sits next to him, and they're chatting close and low, hear?"

"I saw that!" Raxi offered.

"I get up to get a fresh bottle, and that's when whatever happened got started."

"Which is?"

"I mean, I was facing the bar, so I didn't see, but there was some scuffle, the table knocked over, I turn around and Vick is standing up, has this guy by the scruff of his neck, right."

"I think he got too fresh," Chevren said.

"Vick tries to drag him to the door, then those two sheepbrains try to grab her."

"And they *grabbed*," Raxi said, gesturing as best as she could while still shackled.

"She walloped Jonno and was dragging him

out to wallop him more outside!" a soldier said. "We were helping him out!"

Chevren cleared her throat and said, "You were putting hands on a lady in a way you shouldn't without invitation. Which is why we pulled you off."

"And Vick cracked them both across the nose," Maxlynne said.

"Which they deserved."

"Then Vick was out the door with this Jonno, these boys tried to pummel us, knocked Chev really good there."

"Someone was gonna get some good time with these lips, lads, and you ruined that, you did," Chevren said.

"Then the base watch poured in and shackled us all."

"Commander, can I get my ladies unshackled? I promise I'll drag them back to the tents, and they will be disciplined."

"Your command, your responsibility," he said, signaling the watch officers to unshackle them. "And what about your other girl?"

"I presume your people haven't seen her or Jonno since?" she asked.

"I only got so many watch," the commander

said. "Can you boys tell us anything else about what happened?"

"She said she was gonna show him," one soldier said. "I don't know what she meant."

"No, that wasn't it, she said *he* was gonna show *her*."

"Show her what?" Fredelle asked.

The soldiers shrugged.

"Fine," Fredelle said. Pointing at the trio, she said, "You three, back to our tents, straight to bunk. I'll go find Evicka."

Evicka had left an easy trail to follow, drops of blood and boot scuffs in the dirt where she had clearly been dragging Jonno along with her. This led to a side portal of the outpost, which had been left half ajar. Fredelle found this more than a little troubling. Not just that a simple wooden door—admittedly, a stout, heavy door, but still just a door—was all it took to get in and out of this fort. They had a watch—saints, that was the very point of this outpost—but no one seemed to be watching this door at all.

"And this commander had the gall…" Fredelle whispered to herself as she looked out the door. It was incredibly dark—her eyes were still adjusted to the oil lamps inside the compound—and the bare amount of moonslight didn't provide much else for her to see by.

But she could hear a man's voice—moaning in pain—and used that to guide her into the dark. Grabbing one of the lamps hanging by the door, she went out after that voice.

About thirty paces from the door, she found him on the ground. Just lying there, moaning.

"Are you Jonno?"

"I'm sorry, I'm sorry," he said. "Tell her I'm sorry."

She crouched next to him. "I mean, it looks like she should be the one apologizing. Where did she go?"

"She grabbed the guy and took him off that way," he said. "Poor bastard."

"What guy?"

Guilt flashed over his face. "The guy I slipped some rations to. We do that sometimes, that's how those boys in the wild get by. She went crazy when I mentioned it."

Fredelle didn't know what that was about. "Can you walk?"

"She busted my tenders but good," he said. "Told me I was a disgrace to the uniform."

"Can you walk? I need to go look for her and I

can't do that and leave you here. Get back inside the compound."

"I'll manage," he said.

Fredelle got him on his feet and sent him toward the door and then followed along the wall, listening for signs of Evicka.

What she heard, instead, was some other man, crying out in pain. Fredelle chased after that scream, and came upon a clearing, where Evicka stood over a man—dressed not unlike the raiders—with the chain of her flail wrapped around his neck, the spiked head pressed into his face.

"What else?" she snarled.

"Saints, Evicka, what are you doing?"

"Asking him what he knows!"

"Stop that right now!"

"But he—"

"Right now, lieutenant!"

That seemed to snap Evicka into place, and she released the chain. As soon as he was free, the man got up and bolted into the darkness.

"Well now look what you did," she said, sounding disgusted.

"What I did?" Fredelle asked. "You were torturing that man."

"And he was with the raiders we fought," Evicka said, as if that was reason enough.

"Get back inside, *now*, Lieutenant," Fredelle said. "You've caused enough trouble for the night." She didn't even wait for Evicka to respond to turn around and head back in.

"DO YOU OR DON'T YOU WANT TO HEAR WHAT I learned?" Evicka asked as she stalked Fredelle back to the tents.

"Why were you even *trying* to learn something?"

"Because I've been keeping my eyes and ears open. I saw those fellows when we trounced them, and it was clear that some of them were deserters. That bastard you tangled with, for example?"

"He knew what he was doing," Fredelle acknowledged.

"Right, so that guy is the leader of the raiders, from what I hear. Used to be a captain at Fort Nanderack. He got busted up over skimming supplies and selling them to line his pocket, and was supposed to be hauled off to tribunal. But he slipped off into the hills, and took some of his loyal boys with him. More young men joined in, and he's got his own little outlaw barony up in the highlands."

"How did you hear all this?"

"Haven't you noticed I've been making nice with the boys since we got here?"

"I have, and it's rutting strange, Vick. Never seemed like your bag."

Evicka shrugged, giving a wicked smile. "I mean, it's not *not* my bag. I'm not as fired up as Chev or Raxi, but I'm no cloistress."

"I don't need to know about that."

"But really, I wanted to see if these boys knew anything about the raiders. Especially since that one had been tracking us since the village."

"What?"

Evicka started cackling. "I knew no one else noticed!"

"You spotted him? Why didn't you say anything?"

"For one, it was one guy, and I was staying alert. He wouldn't have succeeded if he tried anything. But he was keeping an eye on us, so I kept an eye on him. I guess he wanted to see when we left here to report back to his bosses. I caught him, and he wasn't going to be able to. And you messed it up now."

"I messed it up?"

"I had him talking!" Evicka shouted.

"Who had the what now?" Kelvanne came into the tent.

"There was a raider tracking us since the village, and Evicka didn't tell anyone."

"You all could have noticed like I did," Evicka said. "You were too busy doting on the dog."

"Don't you badmouth the dog," Kelvanne said.

"Anyway, he was still outside the camp watching, I went and grabbed him, and was pressing him for information."

Fredelle looked to Kelvanne, mostly for some solidarity. "She was torturing him, chain wrapped around his arm, almost popping his shoulder out."

"And he told me where the raiders' camp is!" Evicka said. "It's on the way to Fort Nanderack!"

"Why were you even asking him about that?" Fredelle asked. "We're on our way out in the morning, it's not like—"

"We could take the camp," Kelvanne said.

"That's not our job," Fredelle said. "We have a job, we have our orders. Finish the tour. We're not doing any sort of preemptive strike."

"We're soldiers," Evicka said. "Just like the village—"

"The village was emergent circumstances. We had to act swiftly."

"But that's what we should be doing," Kelvanne offered.

"That's not our mission. You want to be some sort of mercenary or something, then turn in your commission when we get back to Maradaine. But if you want to be soldiers in the King's Army, you follow orders, and our orders are to travel to the troops, put on short skirts, and do a stupid show for the boys. You think we shouldn't have those orders, take it up with a general. Or the king."

"Maybe I will," Kelvanne said. "Because it's what we should be doing."

"Where's the camp?" Fredelle asked.

Evicka grinned. "We take the Golsin Ridge Road, just like we could to get to Fort Nanderack, and once we get past Ulter Pass, we go south into hills, and the camp is nestled in a valley right there. The ten of us could easily ambush them."

Fredelle went to her maps, looking at the route Evicka described. Golsin Ridge Road, of course, was marked NO on the captain's map. But it was the faster route to Nanderack, as the road around the mountain easily added an extra two days. "You're right, I can see exactly where it ought to be."

"I told you!"

Fredelle rolled up her maps. "I'll bring this to the watch commander. He can decide what to do with it."

"What?" Evicka shouted.

"You can't be serious, Fred," Kelvanne said.

"We're better than this!" Evicka said. "Why won't you let us be?"

"You know, you're always the one talking about how we're soldiers, that we should be treated as such," Fredelle said. "That goes both ways. Soldiers follow orders. Soldiers report to their superiors, they don't just go off on their own. You got good intelligence here, Vick. And now we bring it to the ranking officer here, and he'll decide what's to be done with that information. I will tell him that we're heading that way already, and if he wants to give us the order, we'll be proud to serve."

"He won't," Kelvanne said.

"That's his prerogative."

"You're going to regret this," Evicka said.

"Maybe so. But it's my call. Now, both of you, get some sleep. Regardless, we've got a day on the road tomorrow."

CHAPTER SEVEN

FREDELLE WASN'T THE LEAST BIT surprised that the watch commander gave her explicit orders to not engage the raider camp. "I'll send word to Fort Nanderack; we'll coordinate some action, but you shouldn't get yourselves in any more trouble. You're already off schedule."

They were off schedule, it was true. They were supposed to perform Fort Nandcrack their final show before returning home to Maradaine—in two days. And given that, Fredelle made a command decision that they would take the Golsin Ridge Road, Captain Olmen's *NO* be damned, and finish the tour on time.

"So why are Evicka and the Trio doing all the grunt work this morning to get us on the road?" Volmay asked as they were getting ready to leave.

"I mean, the usually do a fair amount of the morning load-out," Theria said. She had gotten a handful of sausage goxies from the watchpost's mess, and the two of them were happily scarfing them down in the shade—having first shared with the rest of the Irregulars—while Raxi and Maxlynne worked on hitching up the wagons. "But not this much."

Fredelle had given explicit orders to the other ladies to "relax and let them do it all," which Theria and Volmay were more than happy to accommodate.

"They know why," Fredelle said.

Argenitte had had a bit more difficulty accepting the orders. She did, but she looked ill at ease watching Chevren and Evicka loading the crates and cases. "I really could help them."

"They've got it," Fredelle said. "We're not going to let discipline be lax in these final days."

"I really could—"

"Argenitte," Fredelle said. "I've given my order."

Argenitte pursed her lips and wandered off.

Fredelle took out the maps again as she strolled over the main gate, mostly to give the impression that she was deep in thought about the journey, when mostly she just wanted to get away from the rest of them.

"Evicka looks livid," Kelvanne said, having slipped up to her quietly.

"Let her," Fredelle said. It was true, Evicka would glare over at Fredelle every chance she had.

"She wasn't all wrong," Kelvanne said. "And you know that."

"Even if what she learned is true, she did it all wrong, and I hope you know that."

Kelvanne sighed. "I didn't come to defend her choices."

"She acted on her own, when we're supposed to be a unit. She didn't give me a chance, as the commander of this unit, to make my own assessment, to give an order. We could have brought that man in, properly questioned him, instead of her torturing him out in the woods."

"Torturing, really?"

"That's what I'd call it."

"She wouldn't."

"Kel, I know…I know she's your only friend in this group, but really—"

"My only friend?" Kelvanne asked, raising an eyebrow. "I recall us being rather friendly last night."

"That's…we're not the same as that."

"What exactly are we?" Kelvanne asked. "I hope we're friends."

"I mean—" Fredelle faltered for words here. "I need to walk a balance right now, also being the commander here."

"Oh, yes, commander. Yes, ma'am, lieutenant, ma'am." Kelvanne gave a mock salute.

"Stop it."

"As you command, ma'am."

"Kelvanne," Fredelle said seriously. "We have two days on the road, one more show, and then home to Maradaine. We can figure out what we— what we are to each other there."

"Maradaine is home to you?"

"As much as anywhere right now. Not you?"

"I honestly don't know." She scowled, and looked back over to Evicka by the carts. "I think we're ready to roll, lieutenant."

Her cool tone said volumes.

"Go give the word," Fredelle said. "We ride out, taking the Golsin Ridge Road."

The sooner Fredelle was done with this, the better.

As the afternoon drew on, Fredelle realized the real reason Captain Olman had written "NO" on the map for the Golsin Ridge Road. The "road," such as it was, was uneven, steep, narrow, and winding. As they went up, the edge of the road gave way to a severe drop, and each mile they went, the higher the drop looked. The other side was a sheer cliff face, towering a hundred feet above them. The road was barely wide enough for the cart wheels, and it seemed like at times it wouldn't even be that wide.

"We're not going to make a good campsite at this rate," Raxi said, walking up front with Fredelle. "Do we know how much further on the ridge?"

"Maybe a mile?" Fredelle said. The two of them had taken the lead to scout the road, looking for spots where the carriage would have trouble. But the sun was getting low, and if they weren't off the ridge soon, they wouldn't be able to spot anything.

"Providing we're guessing where we are on the map correctly, and that the map is correct," she said.

"True," Kelvanne said. "Keep an eye, I'm going to check on Delcoria."

Delcoria was leading the front wagon, guiding the horses gently while walking in front of them. Argenitte had the unenviable spot of the driver seat, while Volmay and Theria walked the back of the wagon, keeping an eye on the wheels. Maxlynne, Chevren, Evicka, and Kelvanne had the same jobs on the back wagon.

"What's the situation, chief?" Delcoria asked.

"What do you know about mountain camping?" Fredelle asked.

"I don't want to make camp on the ridge like this," Delcoria said. "But between that and trying to move in the dark, it's the better choice."

"Can we do it safely?"

"I can't guarantee you that, boss," Delcoria said. "But I do know these horses are tired and skittish. They don't have much more in them right now."

"So we need to stop soon, regardless?"

"That's your call, lieutenant," Delcoria said. "But if it were my command, then I would."

"And it's the right one," Fredelle said. She tried to look around the wagon, to see the team behind it, but the sharp curve of the road, combined with how narrow it was, made even seeing the others impossible. "Argenitte?" she called out.

"Yes, ma'am?"

"Give word to the girls back there, we go another half hour, and then we make camp, regardless of where we are."

"Yes, ma'am," she said, tying her reins to the seat. She started to stand up, and scowled. "What's Raxi saying?"

Fredelle turned to see Raxi running toward them and shouting something, but before Fredelle could even make out what she was saying, something flew out. Raxi was clocked in the head and fell to the ground.

Then Fredelle saw it: six scrappy men with swords and crossbows coming down the road at them.

"Ambush!" she shouted, turning back to the squad. "We've got a fight coming!"

She couldn't see the back wagon, but she heard a shout of surprise, saw a flash of blue fly over the edge. Someone had fallen off the road.

Or been knocked off.

Fredelle already had her staff in hand—she had been walking with it—and Argenitte threw Delcoria her sword.

"You pull Raxi out," Fredelle ordered. "Then back me up."

Behind her, she heard shouts and cries, metal against metal or wood. The fight was behind them and in front. They had been pinned in, no place to go. They would have to fight their way out.

Six men in front. If she could clear them out, they could get past and escape.

Fredelle dove in, trying to quickly disable these men, but they were fast and savage. She could barely hold her own against them, parrying the attacks of four of them. She was only blocking, keeping them off of her with no chance to strike back at all.

And the other two were going at Raxi. Delcoria tried to fight them off, but she couldn't manage that and pull Raxi out of harm's way.

Then she saw him: the leader from the other day. He strode around the corner, an evil grin spreading across his face.

He joined the fight, and between him and the other four coming at her, it took every ounce of skill and attention to hold them all off. She parried and blocked with maddening speed; her life depended on it.

From behind her, she heard more cries, more fighting. The dog barking. Argenitte screaming.

That scream drew her focus, just for a second, as she turned her head and missed a parry.

She missed.

The blade knocked her in the side, she could

feel it tear into her as she stumbled to the side, close to the edge. Then something else hit her over the head.

It all went black, the dog barking wildly the last thing she could hear before she lost all senses.

CHAPTER EIGHT

S HE COULD HEAR THE DOG.

She fought her way through the thick black of nothingness, with the dog's barks and whines the only thing guiding her back into reality. Back to awareness.

Then the pain came next. Tearing through her side. Screaming from her ankle. Drumming through her head.

Her head was the worst of all. It made all her thoughts drag and crawl, unable to find their way together. Memories couldn't form. What had happened? Shouts, cry, attack. Something struck her. Then…darkness.

The darkness was easier. She wanted to fall back into it.

The dog kept barking.

She forced herself to pull her thoughts out of the black, enough to open her eyes.

It was still dark.

No, night.

The dog was barking from above her.

She could hardly see anything, her eyes taking their time to adjust to the starlight. The dog—all she could see were his eyes and patches of white fur. He kept barking at her.

"What?" she asked, her voice a hoarse croak.

His only answer was another bark, and a whine. He looked away, and then back to her.

"Get help," she said. "Help!"

He wandered away from the edge for a moment.

Edge. The Golsin Ridge Road. She must have fallen over the edge in the attack.

Attack. They had been attacked.

And she went over the edge, and was now… where was she?

She wasn't on the ground. That was too far down, she remembered that. If she had fallen that far, she would be dead. She was in too much pain to be dead.

She seemed to be on a tree branch, near a rock outcropping. She had somehow managed to land on that, and in the process…

She touched her side. Wet. Blood, most likely. She had gotten torn up. In the fight? In the fall? Which was where her head was hit?

Her head had been hit. She was certain about that.

And her foot had gotten tangled in something, and that had twisted it in a painful direction.

The dog came back and looked down at her, and barked again.

"What?" she called up. "Get help, come on!"

He barked again.

Blazes.

Did that mean there was no help? There was just her, down here, alone.

Part of her wanted to just sink back down into the darkness. Saints, it would be so easy to just close her eyes and let herself drift off to whatever reward or punishment awaited her.

You know damned well which one it's going to be.

The dog kept barking at her.

He wasn't going to let her sink down.

Because he was alone up there, just as she was alone down here.

If she was alone, that meant the others were all dead or gone. If they weren't, then they were in worse shape than she was.

"I'm coming, buddy," she said, and forced her body to move.

She didn't know how long it took her—it felt like an hour, it felt like a lifetime—just to dislodge herself from the tree branches and get herself situated on the little outcropping. Once there, she could take a moment to catch her breath. Assess herself.

She touched the wound on her side gingerly. It was still seeping blood. She stripped off her uniform coat and overshirt, using the latter to wrap around her waist to bandage it best she could from down here.

Now that she was moving, the dog wasn't barking at her, but he did keep coming to the ledge to watch her with nervous expectation.

Her ankle was in bad shape, but now that she got to look at it properly, at least it wasn't twisted in some unnatural way or obviously broken. It hurt like blazes, though. She snapped some branches off and splinted her ankle, tying her uniform coat around it.

All she could do from down here.

She needed water, and her head was pounding. But the water was up there. Other supplies as well. To survive, she needed to get to the top. The dog needed her to get to the top.

Summoning every ounce of will and strength her body allowed her to have, she found a finger-hold in the rock face and pulled herself up.

The pain wanted to be unbearable, but she insisted on bearing it.

The dog gave her an encouraging bark.

"Yeah, I'm coming," she muttered.

Foot found a spot, then another handhold, then another foot—oh rutting *saints* that hurt—then hand. Inch by inch, moment by moment, she made herself find her way up the rock. She had no choice; she had to make it up. She had to keep pushing.

The sun rose on her, a warm glow of pinks and golds, which first gave her hope, but then let her see how far she'd fall if she slipped.

The sweat on her palms, the tremble in her legs—it would be so easy to slip.

But by every saint, by every single person who bore her family name before her, by the soldiers who died at New Fencal, at Gilago Beach, holding the wall at New Marikar. The ones in Hertik Cove, by great blessings. They fought and died so that Druthal would stand, and here she was, a soldier in the Druth Army, and she would not fail and die now.

The dog barked again.

"That's right," she said. "You and me, we're going to make it."

She kept at it. Inches to go. One hand over the ledge. Then the other. Her feet scrambled to find purchase to push her the rest of the way. Her bad foot found something, and she pushed up, and the pain screamed at her, making it slip. She almost slid back over the edge, but the dog was there. He clamped his jaws on her belt and helped pull her back up onto the ridge.

"Thanks, buddy," she whispered as she lay on the ground, taking a moment to find her breath, find her sense. She touched her side one more time, felt the shirt was now soaked with blood. She didn't have time to waste. She put her hands on the wet ground to push herself to her feet.

Wet.

The ground was soaked with blood.

And it wasn't hers.

AS SHE GOT UP, SHE SAW THE HORROR OF THE massacre here. She was in between the two wagons, and there on the ground were Theria and Volmay, both of them stabbed and smashed so much they were barely recognizable. They weren't just killed; hurricanes of rage had crashed onto their bodies.

The dog sniffed at them and whined.

"Anyone else, buddy?" she asked.

She went to the back wagon, finding two more bodies that were so torn apart, she couldn't even guess who they were. The horses had been killed as well. The wagon itself had been ransacked, but she found at least one full canteen, guzzling down all the water as fast as her body would let her.

She limped over to the first wagon, then crawled through it, to come out to find another unidentifiable woman cut to ribbons, her body left with the dead horses.

The men who did this had been full of hate.

And then she saw her.

Fredelle.

Saints above and sinners below, they hadn't had the decency to merely kill her. They tortured her, forced her to die in agony.

She was pinned onto the rock face, spikes hammered through her hands. Her uniform had been torn to pieces, her belly cut open so all her insides had spilled out onto the ground. Her face had been bashed in so badly, it was only because of her long chestnut hair in a braid that she was recognizable at all.

But she would have known Fredelle anywhere.

She went over to her, touching the face of this lifeless husk that had been left here on display as a hateful message. "I'm sorry," she whispered. "I'll make them pay."

And as hot tears poured down Kelvanne Brownson's face, she swore to every saint and sinner who would listen to her that she would do exactly that.

KELVANNE SET HER PRIORITIES: TEND to herself, tend to the dead, tend to vengeance.

Tending to herself involved first going through what remained in the wagons, finding their travel supplies. Delcoria kept a decent Yellowshield kit packed, and fortunately the raiders hadn't taken it. Proper bandages, cleansing tinctures, and several doses of *doph* that would let her actually walk on her twisted ankle without hurting too much.

She found scraps of food—bread and cheese and dried lamb—that she shared with the dog. She did enough for herself that she was able to handle the next task.

The first step was moving everything that could be salvaged into the first wagon. Not that she could make any use of either wagon, but she needed to give herself a sense of order, a sense of structure, just to keep herself from going mad with rage and mourning.

Once that was set, she got to work moving the bodies into the empty carriage.

She knew she wasn't the person to give any justice to the spiritual needs of these ladies. None of them deserved to die in such a horrible way, and she'd do what she could to give them vengeance, but she was no cloistress. She didn't know where any of them stood in their beliefs.

Saints, they were so horribly mangled, she wasn't even sure who three of the bodies were. The villains had been that cruel, that loathsome. She dutifully moved each one into the wagon, giving them as much dignity as could be managed, offering prayers to Saint Julian and Saint Fenson as she did. She had never been much of one for prayers, but in this moment, what else could she do?

Fredelle's was the hardest. Not just because they had crucified her into the rock—it took Kelvanne hours to get her down—but because every time she looked at Fredelle's face, she started crying again.

"You were supposed to be better than this," she said as she took her off the wall. "You were the one who was better than all of this. You were the one who should have fought them all off." She slumped down to the ground. "I should have been there next to you. Had your back. Together we could have…"

"We could have, I don't know, had a chance to find out what we were going to be." Wiping the tears off her face, she continued. "Instead I got knocked off the ledge like a fool. They…they must have surprised me from behind. Never even saw them coming. Some soldier I am."

"But *you,* Fredelle Pence. You had been a Tarian. You had been a warrior, a defender. You should have…you would have been the best of us. It should have been me like this, and you here to avenge me. Then I could rest, knowing it was done properly. I don't know if I'm going to give you your rest, Fredelle. But I will damn well try."

The bodies loaded in the wagon, she said another prayer as best she could for their souls. She didn't even know which souls she needed blessings for. Theria, Volmay, and Fredelle were dead, and she gave prayers to Saint Fenson for their rest and grace. For the others—Evicka, Delcoria, Argenitte, Maxlynne, Chevren, and Raxi—three were dead, and three were gone. She gave prayers again for those who might be dead, and who might be alive.

Then she lit the wagon on fire, and committed their bodies to the smoke and ash. That had been the way it was done back home in Oblune, though it may not have been the way these ladies would have wanted. But it was the only thing she could do up here on the ridge.

She couldn't do a damn thing about the horses, though. She had to leave them where they fell.

She had found signs that maybe some of the ladies were taken prisoner, taken off with the raiders. Instinct told her it was the Trio—Maxlynne, Chevren, and Raxi—the ladies who caught the men's eye the most, and the ladies who had the least fight in them. Those three could have been subdued, and those raiders would want to take them back to the camp. Want to do different unspeakable things to them.

It made sense. Delcoria, Argenitte—she never cared for those two, but they would surely fight righteously against these villains. And Evicka—Kelvanne had been walking in the back with Evicka when the attack hit, and back there was where she had found the most mangled body of all. Surely Evicka had fought those bastards with all the fire and rage of the blazes, and they made her pay for it.

But the Trio, she could see them surrendering. She could see them getting captured and dragged off.

If those three were still alive, she would come for them.

And for the dead, she would come for those that had killed them.

—

KELVANNE HAD ALWAYS BEEN RAISED TO BE A soldier. Her great-grandfather had been one of the Twenty Druth Men on New Fencal, a pikeman who stood and held at the beach, keeping back the onslaught of a thousand Poasian soldiers to let the nobles and civilians escape. Her grandfather fought at Gilago Beach, held the wall at New Marikar. Her father served the Oblune 5th Pikemen with distinction up to the end of the war, even being part of the troops who drove off the Poasians at Hertik Cove. Brownsons had been pikemen for generations, wearing the uniforms of the Druth Army, of the Kingdom of Oblune, of the Braighian Order.

It was a proud tradition of the Brownson family. Her father wasn't going to let the fact that his only child was a daughter stop that tradition.

She had no memory of a time that she wasn't training in the Oblunic pike. She had been taught in the fighting arts since she could hold a stick. Her father would joke that she was born with a pike in her hand.

If she would die with it in her hand, like her great-grandfather had at New Fencal, she could accept it. And if this fight she was gearing up for was the one she died at, so be it.

Her gear for this was critical. She didn't have too much to work with. Her own travel uniform had been wrecked, between the fall and using it to patch herself up. That wouldn't do. So she needed to pull something out of the trunks for the shows.

The show uniforms were terrible, but at least they were terrible in different ways. She started to put something together for her to wear from different outfits of the other ladies when she realized what she needed to do.

Delcoria's blouse fit well, as did Theria's breeches, and those made her feel decently covered. Evicka's boots, Volmay's gloves. Argenitte's cap. Maxlynne's bracers. Raxi's belt. Chevren's facepaint to line her eyes.

And Fredelle's coat.

She'd wear a little of each of her fellow Irregulars into battle. In this fight, she would honor all of them.

Finally, her own honor: her pike.

She was astounded the raiders had ignored the weapons. Maybe they presumed them to be show pieces, props. But her pike had been in her family for sixty years. The blade was forged of Oblunic steel, by her great-uncle Colvin, edge like a razor. The wood from an ash tree grown on her family's property, land granted to them for their service.

The Oblune pike was not what the old Kieran legions would have called a "proper" pike—those enormous monstrosities would never serve for the style of the pikefighters of old that had become the Braighian Order, that then became the core of the Oblune Army, and finally the Pikemen of the Druth Army. Seven feet long, with a sharp flared axe-head on one end, a metal point on the other. Perfectly crafted, perfectly balanced, designed to be used in the ultimate marriage of reach, speed, and power. In a pikemaster's hands—in her hands —it was a devastatingly effective weapon.

She loaded a pack with water canteens, a bit of food, and the Yellowshield kit, especially the last doses of *doph*. She had also found that one of the ladies—she suspected it was Volmay, but who knew—had a few doses of Soldier's Fist hidden away in one of the trunks. That was dangerous stuff; she had heard stories of plenty of soldiers who had taken too much, and it made their hearts burst. Or they hadn't even realized they had been mortally wounded until they fell down dead. But with it she could be stronger, faster, tougher. Put up a harder fight, killing all of the bastards who killed her friends, her compatriots. If it gave her the edge she needed to win the fight, so be it.

She finished off packing her supplies with her own kit for tending to her weapon, a lensescope, camp roll, a fire kit, and Fredelle's map. By the looks of the map, she could make Fort Nanderack in a day.

She had no intention of going to Fort Nanderack, though.

"You coming with me, buddy?" she asked the dog. "It's not going to be fun, or safe."

The dog answered by looking up at her and wagging his tail.

Who was she kidding, he was following her anywhere.

"So be it," she said. "Let's get to the hunt."

CHAPTER TEN

K ELVANNE DIDN'T HAVE MUCH EXPERIENCE with tracking, especially through a mountain forest environment—the Oblune countryside was rolling hills of orchards and vineyards—but fortunately these bastards had made very little effort to hide their journey.

She followed along their trail—which kept her on the Golsin Ridge Road—until she reached the Ulter Pass. That's where the raiders turned south, just like she suspected they would. Evicka's information was proving correct: the raiders' camp was probably down in that valley.

Which also meant the raiders had come out and pinned them in on the ridge intentionally. They had been targeted.

It might have just been that fellow Evicka had caught and questioned. He had run home and told the others they were coming, and they were already mad enough after losing the last fight. But Fredelle had told the base commander about the information, and had told him they were going to take the Golsin Ridge. Was it possible he betrayed them? He was working with the raiders? Evicka had told her something when they were walking in the back, that the raider boss had been a disgraced officer. Most of the raiders were likely deserters who had taken to the mountains. Odds were they still had a few friends at Watchpost Ten or Fort Nanderack.

All the more reason not to head to either place, but to take the fight to them.

Also all the more reason to survive that fight, so she could report on the bastards when she got back to civilization.

Home to Mardaine, Fredelle had said. It was hard to think of that city as home. It was hard to think of anywhere as home. The Brownson home, that patch of perfect land in the Oblunic countryside, Mother had to sell that off to pay for doctors and medicine for Pop. The last letter she had received—and this was many weeks ago—said that they were living in a small flop above a meat smoker shop in Wenikar. Mother worked the counter for the shop most days, and Pop...

Pop wasn't getting any better. Odds were, by now he had totally succumbed.

And she had been stuck on this stupid tour.

The last thing he had said to her was, "I guess this is the closest they'll let you be to a real soldier."

Down that trail, heading south into the valley, were those pitiful excuses of men who had been allowed to be real soldiers. Those bastards had killed her company, taken some of them prisoner, and she wasn't about to let that go unpaid.

"We've rested enough," she told the dog. "Let's keep moving."

He responded with a bark, but not the friendly, playful one he usually gave her. This one was a growl, and she quickly realized why.

"Holy saints, it's that crazy slan from the village," a gruff voice said.

She spun, and coming down the ridge road were three of the raiders, all looking shocked to see her.

"I thought Jordi said she and the rest were dead."

"She look dead?"

"Far from," she said, sliding her hand down her pike to extend her reach. "Despite your friends' pathetic efforts."

"Well, let's show you some better efforts," the one in the center said, and all three drew their swords.

Kelvanne gave no quarter, whipping her pike around over her head in a flash and then bringing it down on the neck of the man on the right before they even started to close the distance to her. He couldn't even scream as the blow all but decapitated him, and he was still standing when she reversed her spin and hammered the blade into the side of the man on the left. He collided into the one in the middle, and they both bowled over. Kelvanne twisted the blade as she yanked it out of him, and then brought her pike back up. The center man tried to get up off the ground, but before he could she slammed her pike into his sword arm, cutting it clean off.

"Ah!" he screamed. "You crazy slan, I'm gonna—"

With a turn of her wrist, the edge of her blade was under his chin.

"Tell me what you're gonna," she said.

His bluster evaporated as he turned several shades paler, blood pouring out the stump of his arm.

"Please…" he muttered. "Please, I just—"

"The camp of your friends, it's down that way?"

"Yes, yes!"

"Do you know if they brought survivors down there? The women from my squad?"

"I…I think so. Please, just help me, I don't want to—"

"Friend," she said. "There are so many things I didn't want to happen. And yet they did."

"I'm sorry, I'm sorry, I just—"

She had no interest in hearing what he just. With an easy flick, his throat was cut, and he was silent.

They all were.

She took a cloth out of her kit and cleaned off the blade, inspected it for nicks or damage. There was so much more this pike had to do, she needed to take care of it.

"Come on, boy," she told the dog. "Day's growing long."

———

THERE WAS NOT A PROPER ROAD LEADING DOWN into the valley, just a trail through the brush and forest. However, despite the fact that some nominal attempt had been made to obscure the trail, it was incredibly obvious to Kelvanne. Dozens of men had clearly traipsed through here, and that had flattened enough small plants and underbrush so thoroughly that any fool could find it.

Which made it incredibly likely that the nearby outposts tolerated these raiders, if not flat out endorsed and aided them.

Kelvanne became more certain of that idea when the forest broke and she saw the camp in the valley.

It wasn't so much a "camp" as it was a half-built army fort. She guessed that it had been an outpost that had been started about fifty years ago and abandoned. These fellows either found it or knew it had been here all along and moved right in.

It had walls on three sides and watchtowers on either end of the open side. There were five structures on the grounds, and a few more tents.

Kelvanne moved off the path and stayed within the treeline, putting Argenitte's cap over the blade of her pike to keep it from reflecting in the sun and giving away her position.

"Stay quiet, buddy," she whispered to the dog as she crouched behind a rock, and bless this good boy, he crouched there with her.

She spent the rest of the afternoon watching the camp through the lensescope. It was clear that while the structure had watchtowers, they didn't really make use of them. The only bastard she saw going up there only did it to take a nap.

Of the buildings, one was probably a barracks, and another a commander's office, and a third a livery stable. She couldn't quite figure out the other two, but one of them always had a couple of fellows guarding the main door, and bastards were going in and out, and coming out looking far too happy with themselves.

Best guess, Raxi, Maxlynne, and Chevren were being kept in there, and forced to—she didn't want to think about it.

It wasn't possible to get a full count of the men in this place, but her guess was more than thirty, less than fifty.

She'd never be able to handle that in a fair fight.

But she thought about that old Kellirac saying her pop would tell her. "One knife in the night could slit a hundred throats."

She didn't have a knife, but night was coming. There would be hardly any moonslight tonight, and then she would see how many throats a pike would cut.

"Keep watch, buddy," she said, making a quick blind of brush behind the rock to lie behind. She could close her eyes until nightfall, and when it was time for her to strike, they would be sleeping, and she would be fresh and ready. She lay down and closed her eyes, and the dog nuzzled her face, as if to tell her she would be safe with him.

CHAPTER ELEVEN

IT WAS DARK WHEN KELVANNE awoke, and for a moment she thought the whole thing might have been a terrible dream, that Fredelle and Evicka would be alive and laughing, the rest of the Irregulars all doing their jobs, that they'd do their show at Fort Nanderack. As the reality sank back in, it occurred to Kelvanne how much she wished she could just be doing the show. She still hated the show, but that would be better than this.

"This is the moment, isn't it?" she asked the dog. "You are a good boy, aren't you? Watched out for me?"

He nuzzled her face, and she scratched his ears. She dug through the pack and found some dried lamb for him, and then more for herself, with a bit of bread. Then she took down a dose of *doph*—she wouldn't feel a thing in her ankle now

—and a dose of the Fist. Worth the risk for what she had to do. Finally, she took the cap off the blade of her pike and put it back on her head.

"Ready as ever," she muttered. "You stay here, guard the pack."

The dog whined at that.

"It's best for us both," she said, as if there was a conversation or argument to be had. *He's still a dog.* "Stay."

She slipped out from behind the rock, out of the treeline and down the slope to the open fort, moving as quietly in the dark as she could. There were a few oil lamps hung in the courtyard, casting pools of flickering light, especially around the buildings, but there was still plenty of darkness for her to slip her way through.

Reaching the base of one of the watchtowers, she could hear a few men chattering and laughing in one of the buildings nearby. She could also hear her heart pounding in her chest. The Fist was kicking in. She didn't know what exactly it would feel like, she had only ever heard about the stuff before, but it was as if ants were marching up and down her arms and legs. But those ants, they were marching in unison. They were her partners in this fight. She felt like with them, she could take on the whole base.

Keep your head on, Brownson, she reminded herself. *Got to stay sharp here, not foolish.*

Despite the urge to run, she crept up the steps of the watchtower, carefully listening for the sign that anyone was up there as she ascended. Nearing the top, she could hear someone pacing around. At least one. Nearing the top, she heard him speak.

"Took you long enough, Corgan."

She hadn't been as quiet as she thought.

She positioned herself near the top of the steps, just out of sight from the watch platform, and offered as manly a grunt in reply as she could. The man on the watch sighed in annoyance and came over.

"I mean, you got my beer or not—" was all he said before the pike slid into his gut. He may have wanted to scream, but as Kelvanne ripped him open to his chin, all he managed was a few quiet, bloody gurgles.

She didn't have time to enjoy that, as she heard someone—presumably Corgan, coming up the steps. She pushed the fellow out of the line of sight and scrambled up the steps so she wouldn't be seen.

"I'm telling you, mate, this batch is piss compared to the batch we nabbed in Yendler's Glen, we need to go back—oh!" He emerged from the stairs to find Kelvanne's blade already in him. She twisted it, and he silently dropped to his knees. He just looked confused at Kelvanne as any sense or awareness faded from his eyes. Kelvanne took the beer bottle from him as his body fell the rest of the way to the floor, and took a sip.

He was right about something: this beer was piss. Not worth it, and she had work to do. From the watchtower, she could see, first of all, that the other tower was unoccupied. That was a blessing. No one there to raise any alarm. And no one in this tower, either. From up here, she took a closer look at the compound. There was one building that was definitely barracks—she could see a few lamps in the windows, and it was filled with bunks with sleeping men. Then the building that would have been the commander's cabin. Shades were drawn in those windows, but someone was still awake, based on the lamplight and shadows dancing on the shades.

A few men were by the stables—and a few more outside the building that normally might have been an infirmary or an officer's club. Those men were standing guard.

That was definitely where her compatriots were.

She could probably slice up the guards outside

that door in two or three blinks, but there was no way she could get them all without a bit of shouting, and that would bring the ones by the stables, and then the ones sleeping would be up, and she'd be utterly overrun.

So she needed a different plan. Draw those guards away, prevent the folks in the barracks from helping, and clear a path for her to get the other ladies to the livery, and presuming they were in any shape, get them on horses and out of here.

A distraction. A destructive distraction.

She chuckled, because the answer for that was obvious.

Back down the steps, she moved through the shadows, along the wall of the compound, until she was near the barracks. She confirmed her suspicion by touching the side of the building—old construction, local wood, with tar between the seams, and definitely dry enough for this to work.

Taking three deep breaths, she ran out toward one of the lamp poles, hooking the oil lamp with her pike and flinging it through one of the barrack windows. Without breaking stride, she kept running to the next lamp pole, hooking and launching another lamp at the front door. Still at top speed, she flung a third, fourth and fifth lamp at the barracks.

Folks inside responded quickly, a lot of shouting and confusion, but it didn't matter. The building had already lit up into a respectable fire, especially around the front door. That burned hot and high—that old, dry wood lit up so easily—and none of them could easily get out. They called for help as Kelvanne was already back in the shadows behind the livery. The men by the livery, and all but two standing guard of the other building, ran to help.

Perfection.

Kelvanne dashed at the two remaining guards —no need to be quiet or subtle—and engaged them both with savage, brutal strikes of her pike.

Neither of them even managed to get their swords out.

She kicked open the door of the building and stormed in.

She was greeted by the sight of five men in various stages of undress. All of them stared at her for a moment, as if they couldn't believe she was real.

Then the spell broke, and one reached for a knife on a nearby table. Kelvanne moved like she was full of lighting, bringing down her pike on his hand, and then whipping the blade into his face. Another man lunged at her, and she kicked him in the knee, another kick to his gut, and then drove the spiked end of her pike into his chest.

The other three made their moves, but she had the speed, the strength, and the reach. She was one with her weapon, it moved by her will, and they were no match. The first two were dead within moments, and the third, she took out his leg with the first twirl, and sliced his arm with the second, and then used the axehead to shove him against the wall.

"Where are the ladies?" she asked him.

"Back room," he said very quickly.

"Looks like you all weren't exactly guarding them."

"Just a bit of fun is all," he said meekly.

All she cared to hear. She pulled back her pike, and then drove it into his tenders. She let him drop to the floor, bleeding out in agony.

She pushed him out of the way as she approached the door to the back, about to kick it open, about to murder any man she found in there, when the door flung open.

Raxi Cresh—cut and bruised and beaten and stripped to her skivs, but *alive*—stood in the doorway.

"Kelly," she whispered, awe-struck. "Are you real?"

RAXI HAD BURIED HER FACE INTO KELVANNE'S chest, wrapping her arms around, and wept loudly. She seemed completely oblivious to the fact that Kelvanne was covered in blood.

Kelvanne wasn't sure how to react to this.

"All right," she said, gently patting Raxi on the back. "We probably don't have a lot of time to waste."

"Right," Raxi said, pulling away. "I just…I can't believe it. I thought you were dead."

"Left for dead, certainly," Kelvanne said. "Are you alone? Where are the others?"

"Come on," Raxi said, taking her hand and pulling her into the stale, sweat-smelling room. Kelvanne expected to find two other women, but there was just one, curled up on the ground. Raxi knelt down next to her.

"Wake up," she whispered. "It's Kelvanne, she's here. She's alive."

The woman looked up, and even through the battered, bloody face, Kelvanne recognized her, and it wasn't who she expected at all.

"Argenitte?" she asked, crouching down to her level. "Blazes are you—"

"Saints be praised," Argenitte said. "Saint Jontlen has come, anointed in blood to be our salvation."

"Just regular me, blood and all," Kelvanne said, taking her hand. "Can you walk?"

"I think so," Argenitte said. "But I'm so indecent." Her skivs were barely more than rags.

"Right, let's do something about that." Kelvanne ran back out to the front room. These bastards were all half-dressed when she arrived, so their uniforms were probably somewhere. She found some slacks and coats and brought them back. "Best I can manage."

"Thanks," Raxi said, putting one coat over Argenitte.

Argenitte looked at Kelvanne again, her eyes focusing a bit more on her. "Wait, it's Kelvanne."

"I told you that," Raxi said.

"We need to go." Kelvanne urged.

"Could be a trap," Argenitte said. "They were close."

"What?"

"No, no she's here to help us," Raxi said. "She's our friend."

"But we know who her best friend was."

"I don't know what this is about, but we probably don't have much time," Kelvanne said. "It won't be long before—"

Before two of the men came running into the building, and one screamed out seeing his compatriots massacred. Kelvanne leaped in at them, making quick work of them both, but they probably drew some attention this way. They may have, but through the window she could see the dormitory was fully ablaze, and many men were running around in confusion and chaos trying to put it out.

"They're still distracted, but we need to move," Kelvanne said as Raxi and Argenitte slowly emerged from the back, draped with the oversized coats and slacks. "There's a livery stable across the way. I'll take the lead, take out any opposition and get you in there. You think you can manage to steal two horses and get out of the compound. I'll be right behind you, but…is there anyone else? I hoped to find three of you alive."

"No, it's just us," Raxi said firmly.

"No one else?" Kelvanne asked. "I thought maybe Chevren or Maxlynne might have—"

"They're dead!" Argenitte spat out.

"Sorry," Kelvanne said. "There were six dead on the ridge, I could only identify three of them, and…sorry. I thought there was another survivor."

"There was," came a voice behind her.

Kelvanne turned to the door, and standing there, silhouetted in the flame, was Evicka Renn.

"Vick?" Kelvanne asked. "Thank saints you're alive, we need to—"

A hand grabbed Kevlanne's shoulder before she could step closer to Evicka.

"No," Argenitte hissed. "Don't trust her."

"What, but…Evicka what's—"

"She's with *them*, Kelvanne," Raxi said. "Evicka betrayed us!"

CHAPTER TWELVE

E VICKA TOOK ANOTHER STEP IN, and everything Argenitte and Raxi were saying was painfully clear. Evicka not only didn't have a scratch on her, but she was dressed in a clean coat and slacks and tall leather boots.

And she had her long-chain flail in her hand.

"Evicka," Kelvanne said cautiously. "The blazes is going on?"

"Kelly," Evicka said calmly. "It's good to see you on your feet. Thought you had died back there."

"Nearly did," Kelvanne said. "Why didn't you?"

"Pardon?"

"I found three girls so brutally, horrifically killed I couldn't figure out who they were. I thought one of them had to be you."

"You thought I'd have been killed?" Evicka asked. "Kel, I thought you knew I was better than that."

"I thought you would fight with your squadron," Kelvanne said. "To your last breath. That they'd have *had* to have killed you for you to stop. They would have had to have killed me."

"I'm sure they would have," Evicka said. "You would have put up a blazes of a fight." She took a few more steps into the room, looking at the seven dead men on the floor, and then glancing out the window. "I mean, look at all that you did, Kelly. Amazing."

"I did what I had to do," Kelvanne said.

"You did incredible things," Evicka said. "Imagine what a proper soldier you would have made if those fools had just let you be one. You and I both."

"Is that why you did this?" Kelvanne asked. "Threw yourself in with these traitors?"

"They were happy to have me," Evicka said. "They, at least, respected what I could do. All they wanted in return was a little blood, and a little flesh to play with. An easy exchange."

"You agreed to that?" Kelvanne shouted. "How *dare* you? How dare you do that to them?"

"Them?" Evicka laughed. "I mean, we talked after every show, and you hated those two."

"Shut it."

"You called Raxi a 'frivolous carnival tramp,'" Evicka said. "And said that Argenitte was a self-righteous, contemptuous wretch who needed to have her mace shoved up her—"

"Shut it!" Kelvanne shouted. She could barely restrain herself from just running Evicka through, the rage was burning in the back of her skull, fire in her heart. The Fist was just throwing more fuel on the fire.

But if this was true, if Evicka had betrayed them to these raiders, joined them, then she needed to know why. She needed Evicka to face justice, she needed to do it properly.

"Don't listen to her," Argenitte said. "We need to go."

"We will," Kelvanne said firmly, forcing herself to shackle her anger. "We'll get out of here, and bring her in for desertion and treason."

Evicka burst out laughing. "Oh, Kelly, you always were so sure of yourself. Thought you were better than everyone else. Oh, except Fredelle. I never understood why you were so enamored of her. But even she didn't last long in that fight."

"Take her name out of your mouth," Kelvanne said.

"And you saw what they did to her," Evicka said. "These boys, they had so much rage. They really took it out on her."

That was all Kelvanne could take, and the fire the Fist had filled her veins with broke free, swinging at Evicka to take her head clean off.

Evicka danced back while whipping the head of her flail forward, which slammed Kelvanne hard in the chest. She stumbled back, gasping for breath. If she wasn't fueled with rage and *doph* and the Fist, the pain would have bowled her over.

"Ladies," she wheezed out. "When the door is clear, run."

"But—"

"Run!"

IN A BLUR OF RAGE AND BLOWS, KELVANNE FOUND herself outside in the courtyard, locked into battle with Evicka. She took several hits to force Evicka back through the door, and if she survived, she would pay for it, surely. But she had given as much as she had taken, Evicka's coat sliced in several places, seeping with blood.

And yet, Evicka's grin didn't falter. It was if, to her, this fight was no different from their regular spars on stage.

"Are you wearing my boots?" she asked as she whipped the spiked ball of her flail relentlessly at Kelvanne. "And your dear Fredelle's coat?"

"And what are you wearing?" Kelvanne shouted back. "You abandoned your uniform!"

"My uniform?" Evicka spat back. "What had that *uniform* ever done for me? For either of us? Why would it ever have earned our loyalty?"

Metal crashed as Kelvanne knocked away the head of Evicka's flail. As it was, this was a brutal fight—they were both incredibly familiar with each other's technique and style, having perfected sparring against each other on stage for months. Kelvanne couldn't get a solid blow on someone who knew how she fought so intimately, and even knowing Evicka, she had never had to deal with a fight where she was truly trying to hurt her.

Add on top of that, the boost the Fist had given her was fading.

"That wasn't even a uniform, it was a costume," Evicka continued. "A farce. We were a farce, show ponies trotted up to give the boys a thrill. You hated it as much as anyone!"

"You betrayed your oath!"

"I was betrayed! We both were betrayed!" Evicka shouted. The chain whipped around like bolts of lightning, almost too fast to see, too fast to block. The chain wrapped around the head of the pike and locked. "You know as well as anyone, they would never let us be soldiers!"

"And for that, you turn on your squad?" Kelvanne asked. "You would turn on me?"

Evicka yanked down with the chain, and she had better leverage, pulling the pike half out of Kelvanne's grip.

"I really wished that you, of anyone, would understand, but I knew you wouldn't," Evicka said. "So honorable, so proud of your heritage. Why do you think I knocked you off the cliff?"

"You knew you could only beat me by fighting dirty?" Kelvanne asked.

"Hardly."

Another yank, and the pike went flying out of Kelvanne's hands, across the courtyard. Evicka started spinning her chain so fast, Kelvanne couldn't even see it.

"If I'm sorry for anything," Evicka said, "It's being sloppy then. I won't repeat that mistake."

She was about to fling the head of the flail into Kelvanne, when a bolt of black and white came out of the darkness. The dog, barking up a storm, leapt upon Evicka and bit and clawed at her.

Kelvanne took the moment to run for her pike, which had skittered off about fifty yards away, near the stable. She caught up to it and was about to scoop it off the ground, when she saw a heavy foot stepping on the blade.

"So this is the troublemaker."

The leader of the raiders, the one who had given Fredelle a hard fight, stood there in just his breeches, looking far too pleased with himself.

"You shouldn't have tried to mess with me, girl, you'll see wha—"

That was all he'd managed to say when an arrow burst through his throat. Over by the stables, Raxi had managed to get her hands on a bow. She gave a nod to Kelvanne.

"We need to go!" Raxi cried out. Behind her, Argenitte was on a horse, leading another behind her.

"We're taking her in!" Kelvanne shouted back.

She took her time, striding back to Evicka, who still had the dog on her. He wasn't letting her get up, and he had her main arm firmly in his jaw.

"There's a good boy," Kelvanne said as she

approached, kicking the flail well out of reach. She held the blade up to Evicka's neck. "Yield."

"Kelly," Evicka said weakly. "This won't make you a soldier."

"I said, yield." Now Raxi and Argenitte were here, Raxi training an arrow on Evicka, her hands trembling with rage.

"You think you're going to walk out of here?" Evicka asked.

Kelvanne glanced around. Between the fire, Raxi's arrows and her considerable efforts, there didn't seem to be any raiders left to oppose them. At least, none that were interested in making an opposition.

"I think we are," Kelvanne said. "Argenitte, can you tie her up?"

"Aye, lieutenant," Argenitte said, dismounting. "More than happy to."

THE JOURNEY TO FORT NANDERACK WAS A BLUR, Kelvanne barely able to keep her eyes open as they made their way through the night, reaching it shortly after dawn. Raxi had taken the lead on one horse, with Evicka tied up with a significant number of leather straps and led walking behind her horse. Kelvanne and the dog took position walking behind Evicka, keeping watch on her every step, and then Argenitte on the other horse taking the rear.

Kelvanne summoned the strength to walk to the front as they reached the gate, saluting the two soldiers on duty.

"Lieutenant Kelvanne Brownson, Royal First Irregulars, with Lieutenants Raxi Cresh and Argenitte Quire of the same, reporting for duty, and delivering a prisoner, Evicka Renn, formerly of the Royal First, with charges of desertion, sedition, and treason."

"Ma'am," one soldier said, saluting back. "Let me fetch the colonel."

Whatever happened with the colonel did not stay in Kelvanne's memory, which grew foggy and confused until waking up a day later in the infirmary in a proper bed with clean linens. The dog was curled up on the floor next to her.

"He refused to leave your side," a medic told her as they brought a fresh uniform to her. "The colonel wants you to come to his office as soon as you're up to it."

Kelvanne got dressed—a proper, ordinary lieutenant's uniform in the Druth army. It didn't fit quite right, of course, since it was cut for a man, but still. It was a proper officer's uniform. After she dressed, and with a bit of direction, she made her way to the major's office, the dog following behind.

"Ah, Lieutenant Brownson," he said as she entered, getting up and shaking her hand. "Colonel Lensing, commander of the base. Very glad to see you up on your feet. How are you feeling?"

"Like I fell off a cliff and took on a camp full of brigands," she said.

"If you don't mind me saying, Lieutenant, you looked even worse than that when you arrived, as did your companions."

"How are they?"

"Lieutenants Quire and Cresh are recovering, and…Miss Renn is in custody. I have received a thorough report from the lieutenants of everything that occurred, in addition to your own testimony when you arrived, though I don't know how much you were in your proper senses in that moment."

"Not the most, to be honest."

"More than fair," he said with a chuckle. "I've sent a squad to the site of the raiders' camp to confirm your statements and gather further evidence, but I feel confident that this whole incident will be closed up favorably."

"Can you define favorably?"

He nodded. "Namely, that you, Lieutenant, did your duty as a pikem…pikewoman of the Druth Army, and did your duty toward your fellows in your unit, and that will go on record as being to your credit."

Kelvanne wasn't sure what to say to that, but settled for a simple, "Thank you, sir."

"Arrangements will be made to transport Miss Renn to Maradaine for court-martial, and you— along with Lieutenants Cresh and Quire—will also return so you can be on hand to offer testimony. You'll be on minimal duty until that's settled, and beyond that…you'll have to see what the army asks of you next."

"Whatever it is, sir, I'm proud to serve."

"Glad to hear it, Lieutenant," he said. He looked down at the dog, lying down next to Kelvanne's feet. "That guy looks like a good, loyal boy you've got there."

"He certainly is."

"What's his name?"

Kelvanne didn't know she knew the answer until she said it. "Freddy."

"Good name for a dog." He sat back down at

his desk. "Oh, you wouldn't happen to be related to a Pelvin Brownson, would you? Served in the Oblunic 5th?"

"That would be my father, sir," she said.

"I knew him a bit in the war years, when I was a young lieutenant myself. Good man, he was. I'm sure he's proud."

Kelvanne fought like blazes to keep the tears from doing anything more than welling up in her eyes.

"I would like to think so, sir."

"You've certainly done right to his name and legacy, Kelvanne," he said, patting her shoulder. "Dismissed, soldier."

He saluted her, and she saluted back.

No matter what disrespect the future would surely bring, whatever inglorious assignment she was given, for now, for today, that was enough.

And whatever came next, she was as ready as she could be.

ABOUT THE AUTHOR

Marshall Ryan Maresca is a fantasy and science-fiction writer, author of the Maradaine Saga: Four braided series set amid the bustling streets and crime-ridden districts of the exotic city called Maradaine, which includes The ***Thorn of Dentonhill, A Murder of Mages, The Holver Alley Crew*** and ***The Way of the Shield***, as well as the dieselpunk fantasy, ***The Velocity of Revolution***. He is also the co-host of the Hugo-nominated, Stabby-winning podcast **Worldbuilding for Masochists**, and has been a playwright, an actor, a delivery driver and an amateur chef. He lives in Austin, Texas with his family.

RECOMMENDED READING ORDER

It is the author's opinion that the best reading order for the Maradaine Saga is in-world chronological for Phase One, and the release order going into Phase Two. Therefore:

PHASE ONE

Thorn of Dentonhill
Murder of Mages
Holver Alley Crew
Way of the Shield
The Alchemy of Chaos
An Import of Intrigue
Lady Henterman's Wardrobe
Shield of the People
The Imposters of Aventil
A Parliament of Bodies
The Fenmere Job
People of the City

PHASE TWO

An Unintended Voyage
The Assassins of Consequence
The Mystical Murders of Yin Mara
The Quarrygate Gambit
Hultichia
The Withered Boy
The Royal First Irregulars

That said, there is no "wrong" order. Read the books as you like, as much as you like, and enjoy it your way.

ACKNOWLEDGMENTS

So here we are with a very new adventure, on several levels. We have new characters in the center, we're outside of Maradaine, and we're publishing in a new way. All of this has been a journey, and I'm thrilled to share it with you.

That journey was shepherded by the work I've been doing on my podcast Worldbuilding for Masochists, and I can't express how much my co-hosts, Rowenna Miller, Natania Barron and Cass Morris, are just the best people to work with. Brilliant, creative minds, and incredible anchors of support. More support came from patrons and fans, like Brian Yost and Ember Randall.

Also instrumental were my usual sounding boards: Daniel Fawcett, forever my absolute rock when it comes to every element of this saga; and Miriam Robinson Gould, the best first reader I could ask for.

On top of that, my family remains a source of strength and inspiration. This includes my parents Nancy and Lou, and my mother-in-law Kateri.

And, of course, my son Nicholas and wife Deidre, who have continued to put up with me during this incredible journey through Maradaine and beyond.

And thank you, dear reader. Because you have this book in your hands, you've joined me on this newest journey, and I'm so thrilled to have you with me.